JUNKIE
LOVE

PHIL SHOENFELT

JUNKIE LOVE

illustrated by Jolana Izbická

TWISTED SPOON PRESS

PRAGUE

ISBN-10 80-86264-17-3
ISBN-13 978-80-86264-17-2

JUNKIE
LOVE

CISSY HAD TAKEN TO HER BED. No-one knew what to do with her anymore. Since they'd cut off her hair and blackened her eyes, she rarely left the confines of her narrow room, and when she did it was only to visit the bathroom or, with hurried furtive steps, the Greek delicatessen directly next door. Here, she would buy cigarettes and the few morsels of food her body could still accept — cake, biscuits, chocolate — then, clutching the packages close to her chest, and with hunched shoulders, she would walk quickly back through the darkened hallway and reach the bolt-hole of her room before anyone had a chance to speak to her. If you knocked on her door, the response would be something along the lines of: "Fuck off, I'm not in," or, "Go away, I'm sleeping," and only in the middle of the night would you hear her moving about, pacing the worn floorboards in her black, high-heeled slippers, or shifting the furniture around into new configurations. Occasionally, the French girl who lived in the basement would visit her and they'd remain cloistered together for an hour or two, talking about who knows what. But I imagine that even then Cissy would not have left her bed, preferring, as always, to hold court from there. With the dark circles of her eyes and her pale skin, and with her head propped up against the stained, rancid pillows, she could have been the portrait of some nineteenth century consumptive, fading away in a nameless and hellish garret.

The only other visitor, and then only each second or third day, was Henry, a sleazy and down-at-heel Glaswegian street junkie, who would bring Cissy the scrapings and remnants of some wrap he'd hustled; or, failing that, maybe some old cottons he'd filched from someone. Dried-up and yellow, sometimes caked with blood, these were strong enough to give a hit when mixed and cooked up together in the large, soot-blackened spoon that Cissy kept in her bedside table. It was as though she was willing herself into a state of deliberate non-existence, unable as she was to face the world outside now that everything had gone wrong and her friends had deserted her. Wrapped in her shadowy cloak of invisibility, she had no desire to communicate with anyone: the fizz and life had gone out of her and she wanted only to be left alone with her sickness, wretchedness and paranoia. And Henry, it is true, loved her in his own sweet way, she having (or not, as the case may be) allowed him to fuck her at some point in the immediate or distant past, exercising her woman's right to bestow favours upon even the least worthy of recipients. Or perhaps she was just expressing her gratitude that he alone, out of all her multifarious former acolytes, had remained loyal to the cause, bringing her his humble offerings and ensuring that the pain and depression of withdrawal did not overwhelm her completely.

At any rate, I hardly ever saw Cissy during those days and weeks, even though we were both still living in the same illegal house. And it wasn't the first time, during the course of a long and tortuous relationship, that she had taken herself away like this. In the past, though, it had always been to some other place — either the country, or the house of rich friends in West London, a house whose exact location was a closely-guarded secret. There, she could disappear and lie low for weeks at a time to recuperate when the pressures of existence became too much for her.

It was after one of these disappearances that we began living together, although I'd first met her about two years prior to this during the period of time when I was breaking up with my wife. We'd slept together on that particular occasion, and although she hadn't wanted to fuck, we'd lain next to each other all through the night, talking about the chaos of our lives in the dreamy, disengaged way of people who are still strangers, but who hope to get better acquainted. She told me about her childhood and teenage years, growing up in New York, Tehran and later Switzerland; her difficult relationship with her mother (her father had left when she was thirteen); her problems with drugs; and her present relationship with a psychotic member of the Windsor chapter of the Hell's Angels. I talked about my broken marriage; my time in New York (we shared several acquaintances); and my failed and inconsistent attempts to straighten out my own life, which at that point in time was threatening to spin out of control completely.

I remember the story she told me about smoking opium for the first time. She was thirteen or fourteen years old, then, living in Tehran with her mother — who, being half-Iranian herself, had returned there to live after she and her wealthy American husband had separated. Having spent the first part of her life growing up in the free and easy atmosphere of Downtown Manhattan, Cissy had not taken easily to the austere restrictions of Muslim society. Although it was during the latter years of the Shah's regime, and the rigours of Fundamentalism were only expressed in infrequent proclamations from Khomeini in distant Paris, Cissy refused to settle down and soon became rebellious. She met an older boy from the American school in Tehran, and it was he who first introduced her to the pleasures of opium (and, inadvertently, sent her reeling down the crazy path to her present state of total dependency). She also told me about the "beautiful" nights they spent together on the flat, sun-baked roof of his parents' house, gazing up at the myriad stars of the orient sky; about how they lay naked on rugs of mystical design, fucking slow and lazy, while smoking the sticky black pellets from an intricately carved hookah; about how wonderful it made her feel to escape the clutches of an over-protective mother, to experience the sense of freedom and immunity that the drug gave her. And all of this with a tone of wistfulness and regret, as if these were the days of innocence before The Fall, a paradise never to be regained — all the more haunting and powerful for being so utterly beyond her reach now.

And it was true, there had been a fall in Cissy's life, something which shook her so deeply that she was never to recover fully: a rupture that was always present, no matter how well she concealed it behind the gaudy masks and chameleon's skin she insisted upon wearing.

By the time her mother finally went back to New York, Cissy had been sent to some kind of finishing school in Switzerland. She'd not become the perfect little Persian princess that her mother had dreamed of, and there had also been some kind of sexual trouble with the grandfather. (She was always a bit vague about this — depending on her mood, the interference consisted of a little light petting at bedtime; a clumsy grab from behind; or a full-blown attempt at anal intercourse, which was repulsed only after shouts, screams and the appearance on the scene of the mother and grandmother. At any rate, it seems clear that the old man couldn't keep his hands off her and that she, in turn, was the guilty one because of her rebellious ways, pretty face, budding breasts and generally provocative nature; all of which was, of course, akin to waving a pair of scarlet knickers in the face of a particularly horny and patriarchal old bull.)

So Cissy was packed off to Switzerland, to some boring, provincial girls' school from where she made regular and extended excursions — first to Zurich and Geneva, then further afield to Paris and Berlin. Several times they threatened to kick her out: for truancy and unruly behaviour, for bringing drugs onto the premises, for sneaking boys into her dormitory — the usual kind of spirited, teenage fun. Then, her mother would have to intervene, usually via the telephone from New York, or on one or two of the more serious occasions with personal visits. These involved meetings with the principal and a mixture of threats and bribes for Cissy, more often than not ending with an increased allowance in return for promises of good behaviour — the increase in funds, of course, only giving Cissy the wherewithal to create even more mayhem.

Finally, she jumped ship altogether and arrived in London

with little more than the clothes she was standing up in. All communication with her mother ceased (and with it, the money), but Cissy hit the party and club scene with all the exuberance that years of repression had engendered: meeting people, getting drunk, taking drugs and generally having a wild and wonderful time on next to no money — something that is still just about possible in London if you have youth and wit, cunning, a personal sense of style, and don't mind living on the margins of society. Cissy definitely had her own style and fashioned her clothes from the remnants boxes of second-hand and thrift shops, picking up on British modes of the sixties and seventies, and making them her own. She would turn up at clubs wearing a garish mixture of Hippy, Punk and Glam styles: silver space boots; dog collar and spiked S&M bracelets; orange, blond, or purple hair; long velvet dresses with stars and moons stitched on; black and white "OP-ART" plastic raincoats; thigh-length leather boots with buckles and spurs. Somehow, the force of her personality, her desperate need to make an impression and wipe out all traces of her own past life, held the whole thing together, and what might have looked a hopeless mishmash on someone else always looked great on her.

Of course, she was beautiful, and resourceful too. Soon, she was selling her own hand-made jewellery from a stall in Portobello Market, widening her ever-increasing circle of acquaintances who ranged from unwashed and ragged dole-queue kids (some of whom she shared a squat with), up to the wealthy musicians and big-time drug dealers of Kensington and Chelsea. But it wasn't enough. Something of the Persian princess was maybe inside her after all, and the charms of living in a cold-water flat, with no heat or electricity, were beginning to wear thin, especially now that winter was approaching. She saw the riches and comforts that her West London friends enjoyed, and accustomed as she had been to having these things herself, she began to plot and scheme, to think of ways of raising herself up to their level, as she saw it. She'd won her freedom — now she wanted to enjoy the material comforts she had known before, but on her own terms, without the annoying interference of her mother and family. Maybe then they would respect her, accept her for who she was instead of what they wanted her to be. At the very least, she would be able to respect herself, to know that everything she had achieved was the result of her own efforts, not because of some handout that was always conditional upon someone else's idea of good behaviour. She had been denied love without conditions; now she would achieve wealth and status without conditions too: she would be beholden to no-one. And so it was that Cissy made the decision to enter the dark and treacherous waters of big-time drug-dealing.

• • •

I don't know where she met Scottish Dougie. He was a Glaswegian hard man of the old school, about thirty years of age when they met (she was then eighteen), and seemingly outside the circle of her usual acquaintances. Maybe she met him in a club, or pub; maybe somebody introduced them; maybe it was divine intervention. Whatever the case, it was a strange, unlikely pairing, but one which seemed to offer her the fast and easy route to money and material comfort that she now craved. Dougie was not cut from the same cloth as the dealers she had known so far — mainly rich kids using their parents' money for a little private investment of their own, one which could produce dividends at least as attractive as any their fathers might hope to make in the City. He had come up the hard way, via the old Gorbals tenement blocks and borstal, and he'd already served time for a variety of offences ranging from armed robbery to GBH. A three-inch knife scar disfigured one side of his face, a memento of some long-forgotten gang war, while his nose had been broken on more than one occasion, giving him a flattened, almost ape-like appearance. This, together with his build (that of the proverbial brick shit-house), made him into the kind of character you most definitely would not wish to pick an argument with, though apparently several people did on account of some masochistic desire to prove a point to themselves, or others. (He had a younger brother, Tony, who was equally as hard, and whom I met years later when he used to buy speed off me in Camden Town. You could never refuse to sell to this guy, no matter what hour of night or day he might happen to call around. If it was three in the morning, he would bellow up from the street below demanding drugs, and if you ignored him, or pretended to be asleep, he was not averse to kicking the front door in, bawling you out for being a cunt and not letting him in in the first place. Basically, he didn't give a fuck.)

So for Dougie, dealing smack was easy meat — there was comparatively little risk involved, and the middle-class kids he sold to were a far cry from the battle-hardened thugs he had grown up with in Glasgow. Undoubtedly, he held a powerful attraction for Cissy, adrift as she was in a cold and potentially dangerous city, and she knew that with him there would be no trouble from difficult or uncooperative customers: no-one would dare to mess with her if they knew that she was together with such a desperate character, and besides, he had the contacts and the knowledge that she needed to get started in this lucrative but lethal business.

Things started to go wrong almost from the start. Dougie had recently lost a weight of gear, worth several thousand pounds, on a deal that had turned sour when some rival from the past had informed on him to the police. The package had been discovered in a parked van at some point midway between London and Glasgow, and it was only by a mixture of luck and foresight that Dougie had avoided being caught himself. The van had been hired under a fictitious name, and with no other concrete leads available the police were powerless to act. However, they knew who was behind the deal and as far as they were concerned they could wait — it was just a matter of time before the net of their investigations closed around him.

So when Cissy arrived on the scene, Dougie was desperate to make his money back, and possibly saw her — young, fresh and plausibly innocent as she was — as some kind of decoy, a screen he could use to cover his tracks, or maybe use as a courier. She was different to his usual pulls: tough, loud-mouthed women used to sticking up for themselves and their kids against foul-tempered, drunken, often violent men. Cissy could certainly hold her own in any argument, and had an impressive command of street language that she'd picked up along the way. But she also had a sense of style, the rich kid's assurance of her own place in the world, that held great attraction for someone of Dougie's chequered background, and according to Cissy he always treated her well: beyond the occasional screaming match, their relationship never degenerated into brawls and physical violence.

The first few trips they made up to Scotland together were a success. The deliveries were made and paid for, while Dougie clawed back some of the money he had lost on the previous occasion. His intention was to accompany Cissy on the first couple of drops, to introduce her to his friends and connections in Glasgow, after which she would undertake these trips alone while he took care of the London end of the business. They would each make enough money to finance whatever side-projects they chose to pursue (Cissy dreamed of opening her own club), and it would enable them to adopt the wonderful lifestyle that she so admired in her West London friends. It would be like a fairy tale, a rags-to-riches story, with Cissy as the beautiful princess and Dougie as the ugly toad who would turn into a handsome prince under her magical and beatific influence. She really did think like this, and in spite of her sassiness and apparent "street-smarts" Cissy was, behind the facade, the original, wide-eyed, little-girl-lost alone in the big, bad world. She had no true idea of the sinister forces she was playing with, and that were about to rain down upon her dreaming, innocent head.

Of course, she knew that what they were doing was against the law and that it carried a stiff penalty too. But Dougie had such a powerful physical presence, and had so many dangerous, well-connected friends, that she found it hard to believe that any harm could come to her while he was there to protect her — he was like a talisman for her, and she had complete faith in him, as if he were the father that she'd never really had. And she saw no evil in any of this. To her, the law really was an ass, merely a concoction dreamed up by grey, old men to benefit others of their own age and social class, and if there were people, like her, who wanted to buy drugs and have a good time with their lives, then why not? She was just providing a service, after all, like a publican, or the owner of a restaurant, so why shouldn't she make a profit as well? No-one was forcing people to buy, it was all a matter of choice and personal freedom — and besides, she quite enjoyed the notion of "living outside the law", of being a renegade. It was an attractive image for her, and she adopted it with the same enthusiasm and whole-hearted commitment she displayed for all her masks and successive identities.

It was on their third or fourth trip together that things went badly wrong. I never managed to find out exactly what happened and I don't think that Cissy was ever really sure either. Maybe it was the fact that she had begun using more of the drugs herself and, to Dougie's extreme annoyance, had become blasé and over-confident, boasting to friends and acquaintances about how well she was doing, how in love she was and how rich she soon would be. Perhaps it was just bad luck. More likely it was some person from Dougie's past, either the same, or different, motivated by revenge or rivalry, who dropped the penny on them. Whatever the truth of the matter, when they arrived at the house in Glasgow at the end of this fated trip the cops were there waiting for them; and this, in a most cruel, abrupt and impolite manner, effectively pulled the plug on Cissy's career as social climber and bon vivant. The uncertainties about the bust and who, if anyone, was responsible were to eat away at Cissy's peace of mind for years to come. When I first met her I had the feeling that she was still blaming herself for everything that happened that day, even though she put up a bold and aggressive front.

She told me about the initial shock of her arrest, the unreality of it all, as she and Dougie were led away for interrogation; the feeling that a trapdoor had opened beneath her feet and that she would never stop falling; and the cold numbness, like a spreading paralysis, as the truth of her predicament became an inescapable fact. That first morning after we met, she took me for breakfast at a worker's cafe off the Holloway Road and told me about the two years she'd spent in jail: first in Scotland, later in Holloway Women's Prison, not half a mile away from where we were then sitting and from where she had only recently been released. Her new disguise was that of a cockney street urchin, with large floppy cap pulled down over her short, spiky blond hair and a long black overcoat that was several sizes too big for her, reaching down almost to her feet. She made such a picture, wrapped inside this horse-blanket: just over five feet tall, with enormous brown eyes and a strangely blunted Mediterranean nose that gave the impression of a tiny woodland creature, foraging for food amongst the leaves and undergrowth of the dark forest. She even spoke with a cockney accent, authentic in tone, syntax and rhythm, that she'd acquired in prison and which, I presumed, had been adopted for reasons of camouflage and self-preservation.

"Yeah, fuckin' Old Bill, sittin' right there waitin' for us — bastards! An' Dougie, with a fuckin' weight right there in the bag, an' the place all staked out — I mean what could we do? Talk about the spider an' the fly . . . But somebody must 'ave grassed us up, right? An' when Dougie gets out, I wouldn't wanna be in that fucker's shoes — I got a few ideas about who done it, an' I bet Dougie does too, an' if I was that toss-head, I'd start runnin' right now — ha ha ha ha . . ."

She cackled wickedly into her steaming mug of tea, and began to roll a cigarette from the packet of Samson that lay on the table in front of her.

"Yeah, but it could have just been from the time before — I mean, the cops probably had you under surveillance the whole time . . ."

"Nah, they didn't 'ave nearly enough to go on from that — no names, no addresses, just a phone call, not enough to warrant an operation of that size, no fuckin' way! Nah, it had to be a tip-off, c'mon — names, times, places, I mean they knew exactly who we were, for Chrissake. A regular fuckin' welcomin' committee it was, we didn't stand a chance — an' some cunt's gonna pay, you'll see . . ."

Cissy pulled hard on her cigarette, trying her best to appear like some hardened jailbird, with her foul-mouthed invective and thirst for revenge. But somehow it didn't ring true — she was far more funny than scary, like some really bad caricature of the Artful Dodger, and I just couldn't take her seriously, she was trying much too hard. I also had the feeling that she was worried for herself, covering up her own fears with this display of bravado, and that she wasn't exactly looking forward to the day of Dougie's release with joy in her heart and a spring in her step. He was in Peterhead Prison, then, one of the toughest jails in Britain, and though it's true it lay hundreds of miles to the north, up in Scotland, she hadn't made the slightest effort to visit or even contact him. In fact, she hadn't set eyes on him since the day of their sentencing. No-one knew for certain the exact circumstances behind the bust, and she had every reason to believe that Dougie might blame her (and her weakness for slack talk and careless boasting), for their misfortune. The slightly worried note that crept into her voice whenever she mentioned his name made me realise that she was actually living in fear of him — maybe because of the bust; maybe because she'd got another boyfriend now, and hadn't waited for him like the dutiful wife he might have expected.

I realised, years later, that Cissy was always running scared, that there was some kind of unfathomable darkness in her which could never really be plumbed. This state of fear was a constant, and although the outward manifestations of it might change, it really came from inside her. She was always convinced, profoundly, that someone, somewhere, had it in for her, that the worst would always happen — and of course expecting it to made sure that it did: she seemed to draw trouble like a magnet. All the time, you could see the wrong moves she was making, the slightly skewed version of events she held to, the all-too-likely disastrous outcome of this, or that, course of action. But it was futile to point this out to her, she would have none of it — she was always right, and all that would happen was that you would become the new threat, the new demon to be wrestled with.

All of this contrasted strangely with her daylight personality, which was bouncy, energetic and outgoing, full of ideas and crazy schemes; and she could also be open-hearted and generous, regularly giving away treasured possessions as if they meant nothing to her at all. But during the night she would often wake in fear, drenched with sweat and trembling from some dark dream; frequently, with a gut-wrenching, primeval scream of terror — her mouth open, her eyes wide and uncomprehending — that had a horrible note of despair and hopelessness in it. It was as if she knew she was doomed, as if she had somehow stepped off the rim of the tangible world and was falling down through the void, cast away into the outer darkness and heading, most assuredly, for some stinking, enmired pit from which she would never escape, and which concealed every shade and form of horror that she had ever imagined. It would take minutes to calm her down from one of these attacks, before she began to recognise the solidity of her surroundings once more, and she could never remember (or never would tell), the oppressive and miasmic content of these dreams. What ghosts lurked inside? Maybe it was prison that had darkened her, or maybe the darkness had been there all along. Heroin, for awhile, had seemed to keep the ghosts at bay, with its ability to make the user feel inviolate and immune. But soon they were back, crowding at the door in ever greater numbers, the drug that had at first seemed to promise relief turning traitor, increasing the dread in a consequent and directly exponential manner.

That morning over breakfast she told me about prison and the people she'd met there, the strategies she'd been forced to develop in order to survive. At their sentencing, she had received three years and Dougie seven, her lawyer having made much of the fact that she was the erstwhile innocent led astray; and, taking into account remission for good conduct, this had meant that she would be released in a little over two years. Despite getting a much lighter sentence than Dougie, though, for her it was a far greater trauma, never having been on the wrong side of the law before beyond a few trifling and cautionary experiences. For Dougie, it was all part of the criminal life: when things were going well you made a lot of money in a short time, enjoyed yourself and invested the money wisely. When things got fucked up — a scenario that was bound to happen sooner or later, if only because of the law of averages — then you accepted your fate: you kept your mouth shut, served your allotted time without complaint and made sure that in all events, and no matter at what cost, you held onto your self-respect. It was not the first time he had been inside, and though it was a much heavier sentence than any he had received before, he knew how to handle himself and was confident that he would survive.

For Cissy, however, privileged and spoilt as she was, the whole thing was slightly more of an unmitigated disaster. She was about to cross the threshold into a wondrous and unknown world, one which contained all kinds of obstacles and unseen dangers; and, as she was taken from the court and driven away in a police van to begin her sentence, all the loneliness and isolation of her eighteen years on God's earth crashed around her in a cataclysm of self-pity, fear and anguish. Engulfed in these cold and darkening waters, she adopted the only course of action that seemed appropriate in the circumstances: she broke down, wept and blubbered, like the lost and fucked-up child she really was.

The first few months in the Scottish prison were the worst. No-one spoke to her and she suffered several attacks, both verbal and physical, from other women who were angered by her pretty looks, or by the fact that she kept herself apart as if she were somehow better than they were, or at least believed herself to be so. She didn't make one friend during the whole of her time there, and she told me it was the most frightening, bewildering and lonely period of her life. There were strange codes of behaviour and rituals to observe; frequently, in her ignorance, she would step across some invisible line, or would fail to respond in the appropriate manner to some request or insult. Her fellow inmates were tough, older women, in prison for a variety of infringements ranging from drugs and prostitution to crimes of larceny, fraud and violence, and they didn't take kindly to some rich kid, so obviously naïve and out of her depth as Cissy was. She, herself, was terrified the whole time, understanding little of the hard Glaswegian street dialect the

women used, in spite of her time with Dougie. She tried, as much as possible, to make herself invisible and adopted a mouse-like demeanour in her attempts to stay out of trouble at all costs.

She did learn a few useful tricks, though. And when, after six months, she was transferred to Holloway Prison in North London, she knew far more about what to expect, viewing the move as a chance to make a positive new beginning. This period saw the birth of her street-urchin persona, as she determinedly wiped out all traces of her former privileged identity, replacing them with the voluble and chirpy manner of an East-End barrow boy, like I said, straight out of Dickens. She learned how to ingratiate herself with others, how to kowtow to, and flatter, those further up the prison hierarchy; she cut her shoulder-length blond hair and adopted a look that could either be seen as asexual or Punk; she learned how to develop friendships and loyalties, and how to exploit them to her advantage during difficult or dangerous moments. Most of all, she began to regain her confidence as she found her place in the prison system, attracting her own circle of admirers and devotees in what was almost a mirror image of her social aspirations before the bust. If it was not exactly a time of great joy for her then at least it was bearable, and by the end of her sentence she had so thoroughly obliterated all traces of her former self that it could be quite reasonably argued this former self no longer existed. Her mother, at any rate, certainly agreed with this point of view, totally disowning Cissy when she tried to make contact with her.

• • •

After this night of caresses and fond reminiscences, I didn't see Cissy again for a couple of years — at least not beyond the occasional chance meeting in the street, or in a club. I had my own problems to deal with, such as where to find the enormous amounts of money I needed each day just in order to feel normal, and the heroin simply wasn't working like it used to in the old days. My marriage had broken up, largely because of my endearing inability to think about the future in any terms other than where the next fix was coming from, and I had lost most of my friends, either through neglect or out-and-out sleazy, unreliable, low-life behaviour.

When my wife left, my initial reaction was to go into a tail-spin of self-destructive, almost masochistic proportions, a drugs and sex binge that had the desired effect of largely obliterating all sense and feeling. All, that is, except for the spiral of barely controlled panic I'd experience on waking alone in a stranger's bed, dope-sick and broke, seeing clearly the entire stomach-turning hopelessness of my situation spread out before me in the vivid, garish colours of a nightmare. At such times, the cruel reality of my predicament was almost too much to bear, and I would lie there as if paralysed, breaking out in a cold, clammy sweat as I suffered an anxiety attack of epic proportions. I could see no future, no escape from this cycle of obsession and dependency; while thinking about the past, and what I had lost, only increased the fear, adding a sprinkling of self-pity and disgust to an already potent brew of sickness and black despair. The only thing that could motivate me at such times, and stir me from this malaise of physical and mental paralysis, was the onset of real sickness with the concomitant knowledge that if I didn't get my arse in gear soon, then very quickly I'd be incapacitated and more or less incapable of hustling for the next fix.

Long-term addicts develop an acute sensitivity to minute changes in the body's metabolism: it's a survival mechanism, I suppose, like a clock or a timer ticking away in your veins. As the level of artificially-induced endorphins begins to fall, all the alarm bells in your body go off at once and you begin to plot and scheme, to think of ways of obtaining more of this precious and elusive drug. If your search is not successful, and real withdrawal begins, you will start to experience a most unpleasant feeling in the pit of your stomach, more accurately the bowels: first, of body-doubling cramps, then a sensation as if your insides are coming apart, as if everything in there has turned to mush and jelly. And this is pretty much the way it is. After days, weeks or, in some unhappy cases, months of constipation (this being a well-noted side effect of regular opiate consumption), nature finally has her way, and you are forced to endure a period of sustained and prolonged diarrhoea that strongly discourages you from straying from the close vicinity of a toilet for more than five minutes at a time. It's as if the wondrous, golden liquid that you injected into one part of your body has corrupted everything within, not just physical but spiritual as well, turning all of it rotten, degenerate — as if the foul-smelling, brown liquid that comes chundering out of the other end is, in some sense, a metaphor for the state of body and mind you have gotten yourself into.

In addition to this indignity, you will also be subject to regular hot and cold flushes of particularly pungent sweat, extremely offensive to the olfactory senses of anyone in the vicinity. The traces of this seem to permeate all clothing and bed-linen (usually soiled and unchanged for weeks at a time, in any case), and to float about your person in a miasmic, foul-smelling cloud of bodily and spiritual putrescence. You will also ache in every muscle and joint of your body, and will find it impossible to attain comfort in any one position that you happen to arrange your limbs into — a fact that will necessitate constant changes of posture, while inducing involuntary and spasmodic twitching motions of the arms and legs, as you try in vain to escape from an inescapable, all-encompassing sensation of non-localised pain. Almost as unpleasant will be the constant running of the nose and eyes, the over-stimulation of the mucus-producing glands, and the hacking, consumptive cough that most users develop during withdrawal. For as the cough mechanism of the diaphragm is given free rein — after being suppressed for so long by the daily intake of opiates — the immune system will fall prey to all kinds of bacteria and minor infections that the heroin had previously kept at bay. Of course, symptoms vary slightly from person to person, and one or more of them may be more, or less, pronounced depending on individual metabolism and physical characteristics. But whatever the case, most addicts would find it easy to agree that withdrawal is an extremely unpleasant experience, and one which is to be avoided at all costs, if at all possible.

My own strategies for avoiding this state were many and varied. They ranged from the pawning or selling of all superfluous and not strictly necessary possessions — most, that is, of what in any normal household would be considered essential: furniture, pots and pans, records, books, clothes, musical instruments, wedding rings, electrical appliances, television and radio sets, stereo systems, works of sculpture and decorative art — through running and small-time dealing, up to street crime and petty theft. I needed about fifty pounds each day to keep high, more if possible, though twenty pounds would get me straight and ward of withdrawal symptoms for ten to twelve hours. Any less, though, and I was in trouble, and three months after the split the stress of finding these amounts of money each day was beginning to tell: I had sold just about everything that my wife and I had bought together, was rapidly running out of friends and acquaintances that I could scrounge off, and my metabolism seemed to be undergoing some kind of miraculous transformation, absorbing the drugs I fed into it like a sponge, demanding yet another shot, first eight, then six, then four, then three hours later. It was a case of diminishing returns, and destitution beckoned.

I was also running out of girlfriends who would help to look after me. According to the accepted wisdom, prolonged use of heroin is supposed to lower, and eventually kill, the male sex drive, but in my particular case this unfortunately didn't happen: I was still chasing after girls in almost as compulsive a fashion as I was looking for drugs. Cocaine, which is supposed to be something of an aphrodisiac, always failed to do anything at all for me in that department, and I always regarded it as an expensive waste of money, particularly if sniffed via the nose. I used to like the rush it gave when mixed together with heroin and injected as a speedball, but apart from this method of ingestion I always thought it was a big let-down; plus, after the initial euphoria had worn off, I was always left feeling nervous, dissatisfied and paranoid. I much preferred speed as a stimulant, both for everyday use and for extended all-night fucking sessions. I also loved having sex on heroin — it took away the desire to have an orgasm, but not to fuck, and you could keep going for hours in a deliciously sensuous dream state that eventually led to some kind of Nirvana when you did finally come. The endorphins would be coursing through your system by then, not only from the smack, but from the sex too, and the after-effects were akin to floating amongst pink, fluffy clouds high up in a Himalayan sky of purest blue — total euphoria, in other words.

I must say, though, that the search for heroin took precedence over the girl-chasing, as the penalty for failing to connect and score was much more acute, and happened much more rapidly, than if I failed to get lucky with a girl. I could easily go without sex for three or four days, longer if necessary, but thirty six hours without a hit and I'd be throwing up and shitting all over the place. And so, in this distorted economy of pleasure and pain, the search for heroin was always predominant, taking precedence over every other area of existence whether it be food, drink, sex, friendship — even, sadly, love.

Maybe my girlfriends picked up on this; maybe they sensed I was a man without a future; maybe it was the fact that my clothes stank and my personal habits of hygiene had atrophied to an almost non-existent state. Whatever the case, the impression I got all around was of possibilities receding, avenues of opportunity being closed, future possible means of support being withdrawn, and a general shrinking in the overall sphere of my miserable existence.

I was also heartily sick of the whole rigmarole of copping each day: first the search for money, then the telephone calls, then the tramping around the streets, followed by the endless waiting in some obscure room filled with other chain-smoking, sweating, desperate people, who had nothing at all in common other than their need for a fix. My five years as an addict in New York had at least provided some sense of challenge and excitement. I was always getting knives and guns pulled on me as I entered or left the burned-out tenement buildings in the Lower East Side, South Bronx and Harlem that the dealers used to sell out of, and there was a constant aura of danger around the whole business that was somehow attractive to a fucked-up and perverse romantic such as myself. I enjoyed the hustling and the large, freely-available sums of money that came my way from the rich Uptown addicts I would score for — living, as I did, in the midst of this drug chaos, and being intimately familiar with every street, den and shooting gallery, and the quality of smack being sold there on any particular day. I enjoyed walking the streets, picking up news on the grapevine and trying to get to the good stuff first, running the gauntlet of muggers and psychos who hung around in doorways waiting for people like me. If I was lucky, I'd make it back to the safety of our room, and the friends who were waiting there for me, with a nice bundle of little wax-paper packets filled with the invigorating white dust that everyone was desperate for. It gave a sense of purpose to my life: I knew what I had to do each day, and I was almost as addicted to the adrenaline rush as I was to the heroin and cocaine cocktails that were my speciality. It was also a good way to meet interesting people from other walks of life that I normally would not have come into contact with: Puerto Rican and Black street-dealers; petty thieves; New York City policemen; pimps and prostitutes; rich Uptown socialites and models; muggers and psychotics; Wall Street businessmen; heirs and heiresses to fabulous fortunes; murderers; musicians; hit-men; and normal everyday junkies, winos and drifters.

Being an addict in London was a far more mundane and depressing business. For a start, there were no real drug-dealing zones as such — maybe the Frontline in Brixton, and some areas of West London, but it just wasn't the same. The street dealers in these places sold marijuana, maybe a little cocaine, but that was about it. If you wanted to score some smack, it was a case of having a personal connection, telephoning first to make an appointment, then going around to the dealer's flat to make the transaction in the safe and pleasant surroundings of the lounge or kitchen. On the face of it, this was all very civilised, and terribly English, but in reality it was a pain in the arse and there was always some hitch or complication to slow things down. Typically, you would phone a dealer to see if anything was happening, and if the answer was in the affirmative, then you and your money would be invited to visit the residence, usually a flat on some crumbling and God-forsaken council estate in Camden Town or King's Cross. On arrival, you would notice with sinking heart that there were several other disgruntled characters sitting around — smoking, reading newspapers, drinking cups of tea — and you would realise that, yes, once again, you were part of some fucking pyramid deal: the owner of the flat was, in reality, fresh out of drugs, and was merely waiting for a sufficient number of cash-bearing customers to arrive. He or she could then go off with a sizeable amount of money to another dealer's house, buy in quantity and cream enough off the top to stay high for a week. Many of these small-time dealers I knew were single or divorced women with children. As the hunt for drugs usually involved one or more taxi rides across the sprawling expanse of London (quite often, the small pyramid deal would evolve into a larger pyramid deal), and as these women didn't get out very much, I often found myself called upon to act as babysitter for one or more weeping infants, while the mother disappeared for anything up to eight hours at a time. I can think of many things worse, but few more depressing, than being cooped up in some damp, garishly painted council flat along with a couple of screaming kids and five or six other dopesick characters. Breathing air thick with perspiration and cigarette smoke, listening in vain for a returning taxi, you live in hope that every footstep on the stairs heralds the return of the dealer and deliverance from this intolerable sense of time suspended, the endless and futile wait for salvation that is the essence of junkie life.

The people I would meet in these places didn't interest me either. Usually clerks, civil servants and secretaries who hated their jobs and their lives, they were totally different from the hyped-up, vivid characters I'd hung around with in New York. With these people, it was a case of: come home from work each day, cop, then nod out in front of the TV with the wife and kids, the smack being just a way of further numbing an already numbed existence. I hated everything they stood for and everything about them, I wanted nothing of their ghost world and ghost existences, and eventually I decided upon a drastic, but worthy, course of action: I would kick drugs once and for all, clean myself up, get a good and personally rewarding job and (impressed as she would be with this new-born paragon of civic virtue) win back the favours of my wife, who had kicked the habit months previously and was now living with someone else.

Fired with this vision of myself as Regular Guy, I went cold turkey and was over the worst of it in eight days. I stayed clear of methadone, or any other palliatives, as these just prolong the process and make relapse more likely; and besides, in typical junkie fashion, I was now just as obsessive and extreme about being free of drugs as I had previously been about getting the maximum amount of them into my system. It's a curious thing, this junkie mentality, this ability to become neurotic and extreme about almost anything. Many ex-addicts find religion, or compulsive sex, or become incredibly ruthless and successful businessmen, transferring their single-minded, obsessive energies away from drugs into some new and apparently unrelated area. I have known ex-users who can't walk past a pub without making the sign of the Holy Cross, and who regard cigarette-smokers as social reprobates who need to be made aware of their hopeless addiction. In fact, you tend to see everything afterwards in terms of addiction whether it be food, drink, sex, money, work, material possessions, sport, love — ultimately, life itself.

Most junkies I have known seem to suffer from a very fluid sense of personal identity, too, often verging on the schizophrenic: there is something fractured in them, something not quite solid. Maybe you see and feel too much; maybe not enough; maybe it is born into you, genetic; maybe it is acquired. Whatever the case, you are always acting out roles, or putting on a front, and you are far more acutely aware than most people of the transient, shifting nature of character and personality. The contrast between the snivelling, cowed, frightened, sick junky and the one who has just taken a shot is quite amazing to behold, and it is this psychological aspect of addiction that is most difficult to come to terms with when kicking. The physical effects of withdrawal, unpleasant as they may be, are limited and finite, and in their most extreme manifestations they only last for a period of seven to ten days, even though it may seem an eternity at the time. When the sickness has left your body, though, you still have to cope with the all-pervasive feeling of low self-respect, even self-loathing, that got you into the mess in the first place. You have to build up a whole new existence, fuse the free-floating atoms of your personality into something tangible and strong, find hope and purpose in a life that is even more overwhelming and alienating now that you have been divested of the security blanket of heroin. Suddenly, you are out of this artificial womb, and up to your neck in ice-cold water, with every cell in your body screaming, "but I don't want to wake up!" And there are no more little rewards, either: after years of drug-taking, your system will have accustomed itself to expect compensation for every little trouble or difficulty you have experienced during that day, and learning to live without this system of pain and recompense is one of the hardest things about staying clean. You are like a baby whose sweets have been taken, you always feel cheated and empty somehow, that something which was yours has been cruelly snatched away — addiction being, in any case, a puerile state, a kind of regression to infancy.

Gone, too, is the sense of excitement, the anticipation of escaping from the boring world of everyday existence into a totally sensual state — which is, I suppose, the junkie's compensation for never being satisfied, for the feeling that none of life's accepted pleasures are ever enough, and that really, there has to be something more. Looking always for some kind of self-transcendence, and unable to control the restless, nervous energy that runs like fire-water through your veins, you soon discover that heroin enables you to ride this energy like a wave — to control and ride it up to heights of self-love, aggrandizement and inner calm that you could never hope to attain in any other way. When all this has gone, somehow you have to trick yourself into believing in life again, into working in mundane ways towards objectives that you are not even sure are worth reaching in the first place. Maybe, after all, you see too far ahead, are too aware of the ultimate utter hopelessness of it all and of the proximate whirling vortex of black space that presses in from all sides, reducing human concerns and endeavours to an absolute nadir of insignificance.

• • •

I soon discovered that my opportunities for employment were strictly limited, possessing as I did no recent qualifications or training. In truth, I had no real burning desire to become the solid citizen, and in my heart I was as alienated from the system, and all it entailed, as I ever was. I was trying to change my life for all the wrong reasons, for some strange notion of atonement and contrition for past sins, when really I was still drawn to the seedy and exciting side of life, to the fuck-ups, sleaze-bags and outcasts who would never fit in. And although my wife applauded my efforts, it was with the disengaged enthusiasm of a teacher encouraging a backward child, hardly the ecstatic and welcoming return that I had hoped for. She felt that she had moved on in her life, now, and saw me as part of her past with that mixture of rancour, indulgence and pity that women reserve for men who have blown every last chance that was given to them in a relationship, and are now suffering the consequences. I was alone and adrift in the cold, unwelcoming world, but at least — as I repeatedly told myself — I was clean.

I managed to get a job in a factory, folding T-shirts and doing conveyor belt work, and stayed there for over a year, almost managing to convince myself that I was happy. I would get up at 6:30 a.m. each day, shower, eat breakfast and walk the mile and a half to work, where I would slave until six or seven in the evening, catching the freshly-printed T-shirts as they came out of the drier. This could be dangerous work. Periodically, the mechanism driving the conveyor belt would break down, and the T-shirts stuck inside the drier would burst into flames as they over-heated. This, in turn, would lead to a fireball which would shoot down the length of the immobilised conveyor belt and explode in your face, if you didn't know the idiosyncrasies of the machine, or weren't paying attention. In fact, some of the old hands at the factory were not averse to switching off the machine in mid-cycle, when some new and inexperienced employee was on the other end, just to see how quickly he would react, and for their own amusement — it was that type of place.

At the end of each day I would be exhausted, my clothes drenched with sweat from the intolerable heat in the place, and I couldn't get the smell of the dyes they used out of my nostrils. But in spite of all this, I felt good: I was paying my own way at last, and I wasn't dependant on someone else's weakness or stupidity to get the money I needed to live. It was also an incredible relief not to wake up sick each day and straight-away have to start thinking about how to get money for that first shot. (I was never able to save anything from the previous day for my wake-up fix, although I have known several disci-plined junkies who were able to do this. As long as there was smack anywhere in the house, I just had to do it, compulsively and obsessively, until it was all gone.)

I began to regain a little of my self-respect. Somehow, it felt good to be working at such a boring job, to get up in the morning at roughly the same time as the millions of other lost souls across the grey, concrete expanse of London, and to do the kind of pointless, repetitive work that I had previously tried to avoid at all costs. I even went so far as to take a perverse delight in it, and this being mistakenly interpreted by the boss as enthusiasm on my part, I was soon taken off the infernal drier and promoted to the position of company van driver. This involved delivering boxes of T-shirts to all the far-flung corners of the city, even to environs beyond, and it meant that I got out of the factory for hours at a time. It was a positive pleasure to ride around the city on a warm summer's day, with the windows down and the tape-deck blaring, ogling the pretty girls on the street and generally acting the part of the happy idiot: three square meals a day, money in my pocket and the possibility of further promotion (Line Manager? Clerk In Charge Of Dispatches?) in the not-too-distant future.

As I said, this happy state of affairs lasted for a little over a year. Yet each night I would return to my lonely attic room where the emptiness of my existence would overwhelm me so completely that I began to entertain morose thoughts of suicide and death. I became introverted and nervous, and soon the only way I could deal with the loneliness was to drink myself into a state of oblivion every night, aided by liberal doses of downers and tranquilisers such as Temazipan and Rohypnol. I listened obsessively to dark, depressive music and read a lot of Nietzsche and Dostoevsky, and gradually these claustrophobic images took over my nights as I wallowed in a maudlin morass of drunken self-pity and endless self-examination. Sure, I had kicked the habit and was off the hard stuff at least, but the emptiness, the weakness, in other words the sickness, was still there at the root of my being, eating away and poisoning my soul until I didn't know if there was any way that I could change this state of affairs. It's the hardest thing in the world to change aspects of yourself that have become distorted and twisted after years of bad living, that in some cases go back to childhood, maybe even the womb. To paraphrase an old Zen proverb, it's like trying to scratch the back of your hand with the fingers of that same hand, and it became obvious to me that, clean of smack as I might be, nothing inside had really changed at all. I was as empty and bereft of direction as ever, still at the mercy of self-destructive urges that I failed to comprehend or control.

(Looking back, though, I don't regret these "lost" years of drug addiction at all. I believe that in my particular case, and for a variety of reasons, they were somehow necessary. My nature was in such a state of turmoil and inner chaos, dating from my early years, and in such a state of unconscious and unrecognised pain, that my first encounter with the drug was something like a religious experience: all my troubles and self-doubt fell away, as if by magic, and I experienced a sensation of calm, visceral warmth, an inner wholeness that I had never felt before. Of course, this sensation only lasts for a short time, the first couple of months of daily use at the most. After this, addiction with all its attendant woes rapidly closes in, and every problem you thought you had before becomes magnified a hundred times. Being addicted to heroin for so many years, with all the things that this particular vocation involves, is like seeing yourself under a microscope: you are forced to confront the weakest, most unpleasant aspects of yourself (and of others), and you become highly aware of all the mental strategies and self-evasions that most people are either unconscious of, or take for granted as part of so-called Human Nature. After years of heroin abuse, you either die or something changes in you, seemingly of its own accord, and you pull out of this spin, taking with you a level of self-knowledge that in other cir-cumstances might take a lifetime to achieve. It's like a sickness that you inoculate yourself with in order to kill the sickness that was already there, and it is for this reason, and not only out of perversity, that I can say I am grateful to heroin — though of course, I wouldn't recommend it for everyone.)

And yet each day I would wake up, sniff a line of speed and set off to work again, happy as a bird, all the shadows of the previous night's debauch chased away by the morning sun and the thought of another day to be spent cruising the leafy avenues of the capital. I had several girlfriends during this period, who I would see on a more or less regular basis, and with one in par-ticular I could probably have built something more serious and longer-lasting, if that was what I'd really wanted. She was a nice girl, sexy and warm, a stylist whose work appeared regularly in several well-known fashion magazines; and, for reasons of her own, she was quite devoted to me, taking it upon herself to look after me with regular meals and trips to the theatre, which I hadn't visited in years. But something in me still yearned after the old life: I was restless and dissatisfied all the time, and it soon became obvious that it was not going to work out. Undeniably, I still had an unquenchable desire to fuck up my life, and it was around this time that I ran into Cissy again.

IT WAS AT A ROCK CONCERT in Finsbury Park, North London, and I had just dropped a tab of acid when a bizarre figure appeared out of the crowd of pale faced, darkly-dressed Goths. This small figure, by contrast, had shoulder length blond hair, a deep suntan, and was dressed in what appeared to be some kind of sailor suit: a striped blue and white T-shirt, denim jacket and jeans, with a straw hat pulled down over her ears — which, together with the blond hair, made you think of fields of ripening corn under a clear blue summer sky. The LSD was beginning to work and my first irrational thought was "Drug Squad!", so totally did this figure clash with those around her, and I instinctively began to walk away in the direction of the beer tent. She, however, had caught sight of me, and suddenly I heard a piercing cockney voice calling my name over the heads of the surrounding people.

"Hey, Phil, where ya goin'?! Wait a minute, for fuck's sake!"

It was Cissy, and she quickly made her way towards me, waving and tripping over the legs of those who were seated on the grass, heads turning in all directions at the sight of this incongruous but beautiful girl. As she came closer, I could see that the straw shopping basket over her shoulder contained a small dog, a Yorkshire terrier, just the face and ears of which peeped over the rim, and that Cissy appeared to be in the best of health, positively glowing in fact. She finally reached me and grabbed onto my arm, looking straight into my face with her huge, brown eyes.

"Why were you runnin' away from me, you bastard? I nearly bust a gut getting over here, an' as soon as you see me you start walkin' away. Are you trying to avoid me, or what?"

"No, no, I didn't recognise you. You look different to before, an' I just did a tab of acid — I thought you were DS or something . . ."

"Me?! You must be joking! Nah, I just got back from the

country, this beautiful house with a swimmin' pool, down in Hampshire. I had to go there to get away from Jed, he went crazy an' smashed up my flat. I 'aven't been back there for six weeks — I'm scared he's still around an' might take me apart next time. Hey, you got any more of that acid? I really wanna trip with you, then maybe we can hang out together later."

When I said that I didn't, Cissy immediately began to shout out at the top of her voice, "Anybody got any acid to sell?!" People around us began to edge away, scared off by such uncool behaviour and probably worried that she was some kind of stoolie for the cops, trying to trick them into selling drugs then getting them busted. At the very least she was drawing heat, and seeing as she had spent two years in prison for drugs, I was surprised at her "don't give a fuck" attitude. But her recklessness and wildness were also funny and appealing, dressed as she was in the midst of this self-consciously gloomy crowd, and within five minutes she had managed to score.

"Oh, this is Rosie, by the way," said Cissy as she swallowed the LSD, pointing to the small, sniffling dog in her shopping-basket. "She's the youngest of her litter, an' she comes from a very distinguished family of Yorkies — she's got a pedigree as long as your arm. Julia gave her to me when I was stayin' with her." The dog sniffed harder and became excited as our attention fell upon it, pushing its cold nose into my hand when I patted its head. "But c'mon, let's get down the front an' see the bands before the acid starts to work."

We spent the rest of the afternoon dancing wildly and laughing uncontrollably — at the bands, at other members of the audience and, most of all, at each other. As the acid began to wear off a little, we left the park and I went with Cissy back to her flat in King's Cross. She wanted to examine the extent of the damage and was scared to go there alone. It seemed that her boyfriend, the biker, always wired and ready for violence at the slightest provocation, had finally flipped over some incident or other and had gone on the rampage with an axe. He had broken every window and piece of furniture in the place, before disappearing into the night seeking revenge for whatever it was that had happened. Cissy had also fled, worried in case her crazy boyfriend returned, and scared, too, of how the landlord would react when he saw the damage.

It was clear as soon as she opened the door that no-one had visited the place since this night of wilful destruction: pieces of broken furniture and glass were scattered all around, while the axe was buried handle-deep in the crumbling plaster of one of the walls. Cissy's face fell as she surveyed the scene, and she became depressed. All her personal things, like ornaments and jewellery, had also been smashed, and her clothes lay in a pile on the floor, damp and stained from the rain that had blown in through the broken windows.

I helped her clean the mess up, and taped plastic over the windows, salvaging as many unbroken pieces of furniture as possible from this chaos, then throwing the rest out on the street. As the room regained some kind of order, Cissy brightened a little and, suddenly full of energy, she decided that she would scrub the wooden floors with soap and water. I'd been eyeing the bed, which was amongst the undamaged articles of furniture, hoping that I could coax her in that general direction and get her onto it somehow. But now the bucket and scrubbing brush were out of the cupboard and Cissy was down on her hands and knees, working with a kind of manic energy, so I resigned myself to tidying up the kitchen which had also been damaged in the whirlwind, though not to the same extent as the bedroom.

Finally, she was finished — and as night was drawing in by this time, and as there was not a lightbulb remaining in the place, Cissy lit some perfumed candles she had, placing them at various points across the freshly scrubbed floor. The effect was pleasing — the shadows they threw across the walls helped to conceal the remaining traces of destruction, while the candlelight softened everything with a rich, yellow glow.

"C'mon, let's go get something to eat — I'm starvin', an' I know this great little Italian restaurant just down the road. C'mon, I'll treat you, it's your reward for helping me clean this mess up . . . and don't worry, I've got loads of money right now — Julia fronted me some until I get things sorted out."

I didn't mention that I'd had some other type of reward in mind, but as we walked down the stone steps of the crumbling old terrace block, I tried putting my arm around her waist in such a way that the gesture could be interpreted as either romantic, or as a sign of protective and caring friendship. At any rate she didn't resist, and as we continued down the street she drew closer to me and soon put her arm around my waist also.

We spent a couple of hours in this restaurant, getting quietly drunk on red wine and talking, once again, about everything that had happened to us since the last time we'd met. With her skin bathed in soft colours from the candlelight, and with her eyes shining, Cissy began to get sentimental about her ex-boyfriend, pleading his case and making excuses for his craziness.

"He's not a bad guy, really, just a bit fucked-up — but then so am I, so are you, it just comes out in different ways with him, that's all. It's to do with his mother — she went off with some other bloke when he was a kid an' left him with his grandmother for her to bring up, more or less abandoned him. He's even told me, sometimes, that no woman could ever hurt him as much as his mother did, an' it's really hard to get through to his feelings, he's so closed. But I managed to, an' really, underneath it all he's a sweetheart, honest."

The thought that this wreaker of chaos was a "sweetheart" with a sensitive soul was faintly comical to me (especially when I thought of the axe embedded in the wall), but I managed to keep a straight face, and nodded understandingly. I didn't want to spoil the mood by being cynical, or getting into a pointless argument over some guy that I hoped was off the scene for good. But I was feeling more and more protective towards Cissy, and undeniably jealous whenever she mentioned her ex. I changed the subject each time she did, and endeavoured to keep her talking for as long as possible so that I could miss the last train home and hopefully get an invitation to stay the night.

As we walked back together, through the streets and alleys of Bloomsbury and King's Cross, with the high Victorian towers of St. Pancras silhouetted against a full orange moon, I put my arm around her once again, allowing my fingers to brush lightly against the smooth skin of her exposed midriff. This time, she pressed up really close to me, and I was more than pleased when she invited me back to the flat for coffee and to smoke a joint. I certainly wasn't going to let her escape a second time; and although I didn't exactly jump on her the minute we got through the door, I soon had my tongue down her throat, my hands on her arse and was guiding her inexorably towards the bed, where we collapsed giggling in a heap, tearing the clothes off each other as quickly as we could. We fucked for most of the night, with the huge summer moon shining in through what was left of the windows, and towards dawn we finally fell asleep, worn out from the acid, the wine and hours of fucking each other senseless.

For the next few days, we were never apart. I called in sick to work, and we'd spend each morning in bed — sometimes the afternoons too — before going down the street to a small French coffee-shop for a late breakfast, or lunch. In the evenings, we'd go to a pub or a club together, drinking with friends until the early hours of the morning, then take an all-night bus, or a taxi, back to King's Cross. There, we'd buy a takeaway kebab, or pizza, and eat it as we walked back to her flat, past the whores, junkies and hustlers who always hung around the station and its environs, no matter what time of night or day

it might happen to be. It felt so good to be together — finally, I felt like I was coming alive again after a long, death-like sleep, and I knew that Cissy felt the same way too: I could see it in her eyes, her face, the way her skin glowed, I could feel it in her touch and hear it in her voice. It felt like two long-lost friends who had suddenly and unexpectedly found one another after years of separation, and I was determined not to let this precious feeling slip away through stupid, self-destructive behaviour. We were both clean of heroin, and in these early days the love that we felt for each other seemed to be enough.

It turned out, however, that Cissy had been using until quite recently, until her bust-up with the biker, in fact, and her subsequent escape to the country. That was what the argument had been about in the first place: Jed was into speed, and with the peculiar ethics of people in the drug world, thoroughly disapproved of smack. Speed was okay because it kept you awake and made you do things (no matter how psychotic some of those things might happen to be); but smack was bad because it made you dopey and apathetic, and it was addictive. Cissy had tried to keep her little vice a secret. But Jed had walked in on her one day while she was shooting up and had gone berserk, destroying the flat before roaring off into the night on his Triumph, looking for the dealer who had sold her the stuff behind his back.

"But I'm away from all that now, honest, I've had enough of that scene — an' I wanna do something, get a new club started, put on exciting bands and fashion shows, an' I can't do any of that while I'm on gear. I would have done it before, but Jed always got jealous whenever I started doin' somethin' an' we'd get in a fight, an' anyway I never had the cash before. But now I've got this money stashed that Julia gave me — she's gonna be my backer, my financier . . . it's gonna be great, baby, just wait an' see."

Such grandiose schemes and ideas were always flashing

through Cissy's brain; but her belief and enthusiasm were infectious, and I really did think that she had the talent and the energy to do something out of the ordinary. Her ideas were original, full of creativity, and when she got excited she was like a tiny whirlwind of activity, hustling and working away as if possessed by some demon.

Julia was Cissy's guru, a West London dealer with connections in the worlds of entertainment and business, and to hear Cissy talk of her, you would imagine that she was some kind of saint, rather than a drug pusher. She was older than Cissy, in her thirties now, and very "hip" to everything that was happening behind the scenes of the circles she moved in. Her clients were lawyers, bankers, media whizz-kids and successful designers, people who had money to burn and who liked to free-base cocaine at the weekends. They were a real status-hungry crowd who saw the drug as a vital fashion accessory, essential for proving to the world that as well as being literate, creative, rich and successful, you were also anti-bourgeois and in tune with "the street". When I was finally allowed into the presence of Julia and her friends, we clashed immediately. I had an instinctive aversion to anyone who made large amounts of money out of drugs — out of other people's weakness and stupidity in other words — whilst remaining detached and relatively unscathed themselves. Julia would free-base on rare occasions, but to have a habit was considered uncool: she and her friends talked about cocaine the way connoisseurs talk about vintage wine, and their drug snobbery annoyed me. Whenever I dealt drugs myself, or got them for other people, I was never interested in making a huge profit out of the deal, other than what I needed for my own immediate requirements. And, right or wrong, I justified my actions to myself on the grounds that I was more addicted and fucked-up than any of the friends I was selling to or scoring for. As I said, people in the drug world have a curious system of ethics. But as far as I was concerned, it was a matter of survival, not of profit, and I disliked Julia and her crowd of "sophisticated" friends. Everything was "darling this" and "darling that", and I couldn't prevent myself from playing the uncouth street yob, so thoroughly did they annoy me. After this little episode, Cissy wouldn't talk to me for two or three days, beyond calling me an arsehole and a shithead.

But we were mad for each other, and this argument was soon forgotten as the summer passed in a haze of colours, sounds, concerts, clubs and restaurants. We went out together all the time, and were rarely apart, except during working hours as I endeavoured to keep my job at the T-shirt factory. Cissy herself had moved out of her flat and had taken a job as a barmaid in a local pub, which provided a large and comfortable room for her above the premises. It turned out that the flat had not been her's after all. The lease was in Jed's name, and since the night of the argument no-one had seen him, or had any knowledge of his whereabouts. Even though we had repaired all the broken windows and bought new furniture the landlord had somehow got wind of what had happened, and was unwilling to continue renting the flat, either to Jed or Cissy, and so it had been necessary for her to find alternative accommodation. The pub job came along at just the right time, and each night after work I would go there for free drinks and food, courtesy of Cissy. I'd stay there until closing time, after which we would go on to a club or an after-hours bar to meet with some friends and continue drinking until the early hours of the morning. I slept mostly in Cissy's room above the pub, returning to my own place only occasionally for a change of clothes, or to pick up something I needed, and as I wasn't getting a lot of sleep, I found myself doing more and more speed in order to keep awake whilst driving around London. However, I wasn't shooting the stuff, only sniffing it, and I still considered myself to be clean and relatively drug-free.

It was during the Reading Music Festival, at the end of the summer, that I realised Cissy had begun to use smack again. She had travelled there alone, on the Thursday, in order to see all the bands, and as I was needed at work to make deliveries before the weekend, I decided to go up on the Saturday, and had agreed to meet her at a pre-arranged spot.

The weather had turned cold and grey, and it was beginning to rain as I entered the grounds of the festival. I'd been stopped and searched by the police as I left the train station in Reading, but luckily they hadn't found the packet of speed that I'd hidden in one of my socks. Now, I was looking forward to being with Cissy again, and watching the bands together, as even a separation of a day or two drove me crazy. She herself was like a drug for me, and I had a physical hunger to touch and hold her that ate away until she was in my arms once again. She was such a tiny girl, almost doll-like in the perfection of her beauty, but fiercely independent, with a restless, rebellious energy that would not accept any interference in her plans. As possessive as I might feel about her, she would not allow me to stifle her: if I believed that a particular course of action she was taking was stupid, or wrong, she would go off and do it anyway, just to prove that she was right, that she was strong and free enough to look after herself. She could be a pain in the neck at times, but I also admired this stubborn streak in her, this insistence on freedom at whatever the cost. The fact that I could never wholly possess her, or control her, made me want her all the more.

I finally caught sight of Cissy, not in the place we had agreed to meet, but at a spot towards the back of the crowd where there were few people. She was standing alone, looking dejected and bored, watching the distant band without enthusiasm or apparent enjoyment. The long, black velvet cloak she wore reached almost to the ground, and she was holding herself with folded arms, shivering as if cold. She looked especially vulnerable, and as I came up from behind I put my arms around her, hoping to give her a surprise.

"Oh, hi babe, what're you doin' here so early?"

"What, aren't you glad to see me? We arranged to meet, don't you remember?"

"Of course I am, silly — but I thought you were coming later, this evening."

"Yeah, that was the original plan, but then we decided to meet earlier — you must remember, surely."

"Oh yeah, that's right, I forgot. Sorry babe, I'm miles away today. Jesus, it's freezing." Cissy was suddenly seized by a spasm of uncontrollable shivering. She seemed detached and distant, not herself at all.

"What, are you ill or something? It's not that cold. Come here, let me warm you up." I tried to pull her into my arms, but she resisted, finally pushing me away.

"Oh, don't get all sloppy on me, I'm not in the mood. Sorry, I'm just not feelin' very well today, that's all. It's nothin' personal, so don't go all moody on me."

I looked into her face, but she avoided my eyes. Suddenly, after being seized by another bout of shivering, she threw up, right there at my feet, on the grass. I felt angry and stupid, and I confronted her right then and there.

"You've been using again, haven't you? C'mon, admit it, you have haven't you?"

"Yeah, well, so what if I have? It's my fuckin' life isn't it, an' I'll do what I want, alright?"

"Oh, that's just great! What about your plans for the club, an' everything else? I thought we were both gonna stay clean from now on."

"Oh, get off my back, will you, you're like my fuckin' mother! An' anyway, it's only a little chippy I've got, I haven't been mainlining, just skin-poppin' a bit, that's all. It's nothin' serious, so don't get your knickers in a twist!"

This last rejoinder was said in such a sarcastic, bitchy tone of voice that I felt like punching her. All my warm feelings towards her suddenly turned to icy hatred and we both stood there sulking, me staring off into the distance, she holding herself with both arms across her stomach and doubling over each time she was seized with a spasm. I felt like an idiot for not having noticed she was getting high again; but she had been clever and cunning, probably scoring during the day while I was at work, then skin-popping in her arse so that I wouldn't see any track-marks on her arms. By the time I met her in the evening, the effects of the drug would mostly have worn off, and anyway she had brown eyes, so it was very difficult to see from the size of her pupils whether she was high or not. I didn't know how regularly, or how much, Cissy had been using, but once you have had a habit in your life each subsequent one creeps up on you that much easier. Although you might think you are being careful, before you know it you are back into the gear once again, and I presumed that this was what had happened to Cissy. I started to ask myself, "But why?", before realising it was a stupid question. I, out of all people, should know the answer to that one, aware as I was of the empty, aching void at the heart of me that only the spreading warm light of heroin could ever truly alleviate.

"C'mon, let's get out of here — the bands are shit, it's raining, an' I'm cold an' miserable. C'mon, let's split."

"But I've only just got here!"

"Well, stay if you want, but I'm goin' home. I'm not havin' any fun here, so why should I stay?"

Again, I felt like decking her. I wanted to stay and watch the bands, and Cissy's bitchiness and fucked-up attitude were pissing me off; but I also knew that if she went alone, she would go straight to her dealer's house to score. I was determined not to let her sink back into daily use of heroin, that I would somehow prevent her from getting a full-blown habit again. But I also knew how difficult it was, once your body has again had a taste of smack, to think of anything else. Each moment, you will be calculating how long you must wait before it is "safe" for you to take another shot, and once you are thinking this way you are, in truth, already addicted. We walked to the station in silence, and as we sat on the train back to London it seemed obvious to me that the honeymoon period of our relationship was over.

. . .

But Cissy had a talent for always bouncing back, and within three or four days she was over the chippy she had developed. She didn't score again, and life continued in much the same way, a seemingly endless round of pubs, clubs, restaurants and parties. I was beginning to have problems holding down my job with this lifestyle, but the boss liked me, and as long as I wasn't ridiculously late in the mornings, he turned a blind eye to my lack of punctuality.

Jed, the biker, finally reappeared, and Cissy met up with him to explain the situation. Much to my surprise, he accepted that their relationship was now over, and instead of coming looking for me, as I'd half expected, he just took off again, keeping his feelings to himself and not flying into a violent rage.

Cissy could be warm, direct and honest, often generous to a fault, and because of these qualities she always had a large circle of friends who would do anything for her. But she could also be underhand and devious, with a streak of greed in her that could lead to ill-considered business ventures and endeavours, and as the months passed I began to see more of this side of her. Just before Christmas, she spent all the money she had saved from the pub on a quarter ounce of cocaine. The idea was to sell half of it in small deals (first adding a little cut), make her money back and have a few grammes for personal use over the holidays, so that she could spend time with Julia in Kensington without having to ponce off her, as she said. However, as soon as she had scored, she started to dip into the coke, and within four days almost half of it had gone. Instead of just stopping and selling the rest as she had originally intended, she took half of the remainder for herself, and cut the rest so badly that nobody would buy it. Then, depressed at this state of affairs, she finished off the remaining uncut two grammes in a vain attempt to cheer herself up. By the time Christmas came, she had no cocaine and no money, and was so down about the situation that she refused to go out and celebrate. Instead, she stayed in her room the whole time, reading magazines and sulking. All of this would have been laughable if it hadn't been so tragic, and another big row followed.

"I told you not to buy that shit — it's always the same, gone before you know it, an' it's a total con anyway. I mean, if you wanna freeze your nose just buy some novocaine, for fuck's sake!"

"Oh, an' you're Mr. Perfect, I suppose, like you never make mistakes, or waste money on drugs. C'mon, you're just as big a junkie as I am, so stop makin' out you're some kind of saint! Just take a look at yourself for a change!"

We were walking back from the station, through one of the enclosed alleyways around King's Cross, and so busy arguing that at first we didn't notice the lone figure sat huddled on a darkened doorstep with his head between his knees. As we came closer, I saw that it was Jimmy, a junkie friend of Cissy's who lived in a damp basement flat in one of the crumbling old tenement buildings further up the street. His shoulders were shaking and I could see that he was quietly sobbing, and Cissy immediately forgot about the argument and went over to him.

"Jimmy, what's the matter, what's happened? why are you sat outside here like this? C'mon, it's freezing, let's go inside."

Jimmy didn't answer, but just kept on sobbing and moaning

to himself. His lank, greasy hair covered his face, his jeans were torn at the knee, and even from a couple of yards away you could smell the malodorous reek that came off his clothes. Cissy sat down next to him on the step, putting her arm around his shoulder, then she asked him once again what was the matter.

"It's 'Rene — she tried to top herself by jumpin' under a tube train, for Christ's sake. Only she didn't do it properly, the train stopped in time, or pushed her along, or something . . . but anyway, it went over her leg an' they've had to amputate it — she's in UCH now, still unconscious, I've just come from there. Oh shit, what am I gonna do, what about the kid . . . ?"

This was so heavy — so over-the-top — that I had to stifle an impulse to laugh; but Cissy had gone deathly pale, and neither of us knew what to say. Irene was Jimmy's common-law wife, fresh over from Ireland when they met, a well-brought-up country girl who always seemed totally out of her depth and perpetually bemused whenever you spoke to her. She was no match for Jimmy with his underhand junkie ways, and was always trying to get him to stop taking drugs, probably praying for his poor, abandoned soul each Sunday in church. Although he'd made something of an effort to stay clean since the baby had been born, basically he was incorrigible and always found ways to get money for a hit, even if the flat was without food or electricity. In spite of this, his weakness and selfishness, he truly doted on Irene and his baby daughter with the kind of helpless, hopeless love that I saw time and again in junkie relationships — a love born out of emptiness and desperation that could break your heart if you thought about it for any length of time at all.

Finally, I broke the sob-wracked silence that had fallen between us.

"C'mon, Jimmy, let's go get a drink — you're gonna freeze to death if you stay out here much longer."

"I don't care, I don't wanna fuckin' drink . . . I just wanna crawl into a corner somewhere an' die. An' anyway, I couldn't face all those pissed-up fuckers in the pub, no way."

"Yeah, c'mon babe," said Cissy, "can't you see he's sick? Here Jimmy, come with me, I'll get you some gear — you need to get out of it tonight, forget about everythin', then tomorrow you can start dealin' with things, start thinkin' about what to do. Rene's gonna need you, so is the kid, but tonight you need to forget. Listen babe, I won't be long, an' I promise I won't get high myself — but you can see what a state he's in, an' someone's gotta look after him. So here, take my keys an' wait up for me, I won't be long, honest. I love you . . ."

Before I could say anything, she had planted a kiss on my lips and had disappeared into the night with Jimmy in tow. I was worried that she wouldn't be able to resist taking a hit also, but when she returned about two-thirty in the morning, and got into bed, I could see she had been true to her word: she'd spent the last bit of money she had on getting Jimmy high, but had not taken anything herself. She had stayed up half the night talking with him, trying to calm him down until he'd finally passed out, and now she was worn out herself, pale and shaking from the emotional trauma of the last few hours. She curled up in my arms, the tears pouring silently down her face as I held her close, and I could feel the darkness inside her welling up, as if from an underground cave. Just before I fell asleep, I heard her whispering, almost to herself, "I can't deal with it anymore, there's just too much pain . . . really babe, I can't deal with it anymore — what the fuck are we gonna do . . . ?"

• • •

As the winter passed, I could feel Cissy starting to slip away from me. She would disappear for days at a time, only to return looking pale and wasted, and if I questioned where she

had been, she would fly into a rage and an argument would follow. I didn't need to ask, anyhow — it was obvious what she
had been doing, and the Whys? the Wheres? and the Whos?
were pretty much irrelevant. I wasn't prepared, even if it had
been possible, to follow her around the streets twenty four
hours a day, checking on her movements and generally acting
like some kind of policeman. If someone is determined to score
heroin, there is little you can do to prevent them — unless, that
is, you're prepared to lock them in a room somewhere, like the
Frankie Machine character in the movie version of *The Man
with the Golden Arm*. If the desire to stay clean doesn't come
from deep inside, any attempt to kick the habit will be doomed
from the start: as soon as your body starts to feel good again,
and your energy returns, you will be subconsciously counting
the days until you feel it is possible to give yourself that "one-
off" special treat. This is how addiction works — it is insidious
and strange, and its secret workings turn like wheels at the back
of your consciousness, providing you with all the justifica-
tions and reasons you could possibly need to indulge yourself
once more.

Soon, she began to miss her shifts at the pub, coming up with
the most feeble excuses, and her position there was looking
increasingly tenuous. As she depended on the job for her living arrangements, and as it was the middle of a very cold and
bitter winter, this was serious; and although the landlord liked
her, and gave her many "second chances", he did, after all,
have a business to run. It was obvious to me that pretty soon
the inevitable would happen, and she would find herself out
on the street once more, together with her dog and the few
meagre belongings she still possessed.

I thought about inviting her to move in with me, but she
wasn't keen on that idea. My flat was up in Muswell Hill, a
leafy and pleasant, but far-flung North London suburb with no
Underground station and, as Cissy said, far away from where

the action was. On the few occasions that she had stayed with me there, she'd been nervous and restless, saying that she felt like an alien in the streets, that she couldn't stand being so cut off from all her friends and habitual haunts. What she really meant, of course, was that it was far away from all the heroin dealers she knew, who mostly lived around Camden Town and King's Cross. I had chosen the area to live in for this very reason, so that I would be away from those streets and the drug memories I associated with them. But in any case, I sensed that living together with Cissy in Muswell Hill was not a viable option: she just wasn't cut out for life in the suburbs. Junkies tend to form dependent relationships with the neighbourhoods they score in, as if they are attached to them by some invisible umbilical cord, and away from their home turf they feel insecure and vulnerable. It's not even just that drugs can be bought relatively easily in these areas. It's more to do with the atmosphere of the streets, what you might call a feeling of "drug potentiality," and I understood perfectly. I used to feel the same way about the Lower East Side in New York, and would start to feel anxious and paranoid as soon as I left the area. I'd experience a distinct sensation of relief upon returning there from any journey, no matter how brief, outside the city limits, or even away from the neighbourhood.

One evening, while I was having a drink with some friends in a pub, one of them, Andy, happened to mention that he was intending to break a squat, and that he had found the perfect place: a large terraced house in Camden Town that had not been lived in for at least five years. He had already been inside one night to examine the property, and reckoned that although it was dirty and full of garbage, structurally it was sound: the toilets hadn't been smashed by the council, and it should be possible to hot-wire the electricity and turn the gas and water supplies back on without too much trouble.

Cissy and I were growing ever further apart, largely because of her re-entry into the drug world and the pressures of junkie life: the way things were going our relationship would soon fall apart altogether, unless there was some kind of radical change. She was now buying smack each day, spending all her money from the pub on it, and was forced to wear long-sleeved shirts and sweaters all the time, to conceal the track-marks that coloured the inside of each arm at the elbow. She didn't even bother to pretend to me anymore that she wasn't using, adopting a fatalistic "take me as I am, or leave me" kind of attitude, with a mixture of sadness and defiance that was somehow both tragic and pathetic at the same time. I could either accept this state of affairs, and let our feelings for each other die a natural death, or I could try to do something about it — try to get Cissy off smack, and pull her back from the brink of this hole that she seemed intent on digging for herself. As I couldn't imagine my life without her now, the first alternative was simply not a choice that was open to me: I couldn't just let her wander off into the night alone. I preferred to go with her and risk the possible consequences than return to my solitary life of meaningless work and mundane relationships, that of course was safe, but also boring and empty.

And so a plan began to grow in my mind, an idea that surely deserves filing under the heading GREAT, BUT MISGUIDED, AND ULTIMATELY STUPID: I would quit my job, move into the squat with Cissy, spend the money I had saved on a half ounce of good-quality heroin and gradually wean her away from her habit by reducing the amount I gave her each day. I would support us both by selling the rest to friends and acquaintances, who would appreciate the fact that it wasn't cut to hell like most of the street stuff that was available at that time. Then, once Cissy was clean, and the stuff had all been sold, we would get out of London: with the money saved from dealing, and from having no rent or fuel bills to pay, we would be able to afford the rent on a cottage in the West Country, maybe Devon or

Cornwall. We would stay there for six months or a year, until our battered psyches had healed and we felt strong enough to return to the city; or maybe we would take off altogether and travel around the world, visit India, Tibet, Africa and the Far East. Suddenly, the possibilities seemed endless, and I could hardly contain my enthusiasm as I broached the subject with Cissy.

"What, you'd do that for me? Spend all your money buyin' smack, on the off-chance that you can get me to stop takin' it? What about you? How're you gonna handle being so close to it all again, havin' it right there under your nose? At least now I do it on my own, well away from you — you don't see it around you each day, an' you're not sittin' on top of a huge amount like you will be if you go through with this stupid plan. Look, I really love you for dreaming this whole thing up, an' thinkin' about me, but I don't want the responsibility of you gettin' back into gear on my head, no way. I couldn't deal with that, babe, honest. Forget it, it's my problem, it's a crazy idea, an' I don't want you gettin' involved. You've been clean for a year an' a half now — please don't go an' fuck it up just on my account."

But I was all fired up, and brushed Cissy's reservations aside — there was no way I was going to get back into using again, of that I was sure. At least we had to go and take a look at this squat, just to see what it was like; and if it wasn't in too bad a state, then we could move in together and save on rent, if nothing else.

Reluctantly Cissy agreed. And so, one cold and windy night, we walked up Camden Road to the large terraced house that Andy had already broken into, and knocked loudly on the heavy black door with its cracked and peeling varnish.

The hallway was dark and gloomy, lit by only one bare light-bulb that Andy had hooked up to the electricity supply of another squat two doors down the street. Directly ahead of us, at the end of the hall, stairs led up to a first-floor landing where there was a bathroom and a window looking out over a weed-infested back garden that was enclosed within three high, red-brick walls. Clouds blew across a bright winter moon, and the house was full of shadows, echoes of other times, of other unknown, gone-forever-lives that seemed to reverberate between the grimy, pock-marked walls. We climbed the stairs and explored each darkened room in turn, the shadows thrown by Andy's candle dancing wildly around the hidden corners in a silent, ghostly pantomime. He had already claimed the large room on the first floor for himself, but so far all the others were untaken. The top floor room seemed the most attractive to me — it, too, was large and spacious, and the paintwork and plaster were in good condition. Being at the top of the house, I reckoned, it would also be the warmest room, and it had the added bonus of its own small, private kitchen that looked out from a height over the back gardens of the neighbouring houses. I turned to Cissy.

"Well, what do you think? D'you fancy moving in here, or what?"

"Yeah . . . well, er . . . it's got possibilities, certainly, but it'd need a lot of work . . . it's pretty damp downstairs, an' there's no gas or electric . . . but yeah, I think we could do somethin' with it. An' I kinda like the atmosphere, too, I feel comfortable here . . . so yeah, let's do it, why not? I'm sick of workin' at the pub anyway, an' I promise I'll try an' clean myself up, honest."

Cissy threw herself into my arms and gave me a big hug. As I held her close and kissed her, I really believed that this was some kind of new beginning for us, and though I could see the possible pitfalls, I felt sure that the holy and beatific light of love, that seemed to shine through the cracks in these battered old walls, would protect and guide us through any dangers during the weeks and months ahead.

· · ·

With Cissy using on a daily basis, all her attempts to keep her habit a secret had long been abandoned. She would shoot up in front of me two, three, often four times a day, and she was looking pale and thin, forgetting to eat, running around the streets hustling for drugs and money at all hours of the day and night. We had moved our belongings into the squat, and I was still working at the T-shirt factory, but Cissy had given up her pub job and we were constantly short of money. I had a size-able sum stashed for emergencies that I was trying not to break into — but the pressures of supporting both of us, and of paying for Cissy's growing habit, were proving too much and it was beginning to dwindle. I was worried about her, too. She would disappear for hours, even days, at a time, and would return looking worn-out and depressed, either having failed to cop, or feeling cheated over the miserable amount of smack she got for her money. I had no idea where she might be during these times: there were dozens of small-time dealers dotted around the council estates and high-rise tower blocks of North London, and I feared for her safety, that she might get attacked, or busted, or worst of all that she might OD anonymously in some cold and draughty toilet somewhere. I decided to return to my original idea of buying a quantity of heroin, then using part of it to wean Cissy away before selling the rest. At least then she would be at home, and not out on the cold, dangerous streets.

I gave two weeks notice at work and started asking around to see where I might score a half ounce of clean smack. In spite of all my connections in the drug world, this was not an easy thing to do, and finally I had to settle for a quarter ounce. With this, I should at least have enough to stabilise Cissy's habit and be able to recover my money by selling the remain-der — I could always buy more the next time.

It was a strange feeling to re-enter the world of heroin

again after so long. In some ways it felt like I had never left, and in another way I felt distant from it all, as if I was watching myself and my actions from down the wrong end of a telescope. As I watched the dealer weighing out the smack, I felt an undeniable tingling sensation throughout my body, and I was disturbed to feel a rising excitement in the pit of my stomach, as if I was about to take a hit myself. I hadn't counted on this and tried to ignore it; but as I walked back through the rain-soaked Camden streets, I couldn't get rid of the nagging voice that seemed to be urging me to take a little taste, just a little, for old time's sake.

We had managed to get the electricity, gas and water supplies hooked-up, and I had painted our room, laying an old carpet from a second-hand shop across the bare, wooden floor-boards. Cissy had decorated the walls with photos, posters and cotton wall-hangings, and had even managed to create a canopy for our bed out of one of them, so that it now resembled an old four-poster or, together with all the embroidered cushions she had, something from North Africa or the Middle East. It was a warm and comfortable room, and as I walked through the backsreets I could see, across the tangle of gardens and wind-blown treetops, the light from our window high up at the top of the house, and I was looking forward to surprising Cissy with the gear I had stashed inside my sock. It seems incredible to me, now, that I actually believed this plan would work: that Cissy would be able to systematically reduce the amount she was taking each day and, even more, that I would be self-disciplined enough to be able to refrain from dipping into the supply myself.

When I arrived in our kitchen at the top of the stairs, there was nobody in. I put the bag of heroin on the table, then sat down to read a book and wait for her. I must have fallen asleep, for I awoke a couple of hours later, cold and bad-tempered, and the first thing that my eyes fell upon was the little plastic bag of brown powder, tied with an elastic band, that sat waiting patiently on the table. Drawn inexorably, I went over and picked it up, turning it over and over in my hand. Surely, just one little taste wouldn't hurt, nobody would know. It would probably be hours before Cissy came home, and I could wait until the morning to tell her about the smack. And, almost before I knew it, I had gone to the cupboard where she kept her spoons and syringes and was cooking up a hit, just as if I had never stopped at all.

Once, in New York, I watched somebody who had been clean for five years take a shot. Something had gone badly wrong in this poor fucker's life, and in a wonderfully perverse spirit of masochistic glee, he had obviously determined to wipe out everything he had so painstakingly built up in the intervening period. Since he had kicked the habit, he had got a good job, married, started a family and bought a house, and he believed his years in the drug wilderness were behind him, just a faint recollection from his wild and wasted youth. He had come to our flat with some mutual friends, and asked me if he could get high there, rather than return to the cold and empty house that awaited him in Westchester, or wherever it was that he lived; and though I was reluctant at first, not wanting him to OD on our floor, I did eventually agree. I watched, fascinated, as he prepared his shot, and as it hit him layers of his personality seemed to peel away. He was like a snake shedding its skin, and he literally seemed to grow years younger right in front of my eyes. The responsible adult character that he had attempted to grow into and adopt as his own also seemed to slough away — it was as if all the intervening years had melted into the air, and he was right back there as if they'd never happened, back on the one-way track to oblivion. I felt dizzy and vertiginous as I watched him enter his spin.

The brown liquid bubbled in the spoon that I held above the candle, and as it cooled I drew the smack up through the cotton filter into the syringe. As if in a dream, I tied-off and got a vein up almost immediately, "Ol' Faithful" in the crook of my left arm, and as I stuck the needle in I almost shit myself in anticipation. The rush was incredible. I thought I was going to pass out, it was so intense, a spreading white light that warmed every cell and nerve-ending in my body, and that felt like the best one hundred orgasms I'd ever had, all rolled into one. I lay slumped in my seat, totally sledgehammered, drifting in and out of consciousness while luxuriating in the warm, healing waters of the high.

There is something undeniably sexual about shooting up, and I'd experience a sharp pang of jealousy if I ever watched another man give one of my girlfriends a shot. But it's like a surrogate sexuality, and with some junkie couples it does more or less take the place of active sex, due to the well-known effect of long-term heroin use on the male libido. Paradoxically, it doesn't seem to affect the female of the species in quite the same way, and I'd often noticed that girls who were uptight sexually when straight became much freer and more relaxed, and had orgasms more intensely, when they were stoned. Some junkies sit for half an hour at a time, booting and re-booting the blood in the syringe, out and back in again, which always struck me as being quasi-vampiric, maybe even necrophiliac. In a room full of addicts, the air thick with cigarette smoke and the odour of sweat, the feeling is somehow pornographic — a sleazy, voyeuristic type of necro-sexuality that is, to a greater or lesser extent, addictive in itself.

I must have stayed in this oceanic state, bathing in the glow, for three or four hours, slipping in and out of dreams and feeling the warmth in the pit of my stomach like a comforting weight. It anchored me, it allowed me to feel the physicality of my own existence, and it entwined its warm tentacles through my intestines and around my spine, reaching every part of my limbs and body.

Eventually, I started to come down, and I began to feel guilty and bad-tempered again. I knew that I'd fucked up by getting high, but what was most worrying was that I had no real awareness of how it had actually happened. No conscious decision had been taken. I had moved as if under the control of some power alien to me, like a sleep-walker; and it suddenly seemed that this whole idea I'd concocted of weaning Cissy away from her habit was merely a pretext that my unconscious mind had formulated for getting me back into close contact with heroin once again. I was aware of a hidden part of me that had its own agenda of secret appetites and desires, that moved of its own volition and took no account of "me" at all. I could feel it inside, working away, moving silently along its own invisible tracks; and not only that, it was much stronger than me — of this, I was totally sure.

I went to bed determined not to succumb to the urge again, and when Cissy came in about 4 a.m. I pretended to be asleep. I didn't want her to know that I had got high, and decided I'd wait until the morning to spring my surprise upon her.

She, of course, was delighted. She had only managed to cop a pitiful amount of skag the night before, after waiting for hours, and was depressed and sick when she woke in the morning. Her big eyes nearly popped when she saw what I'd bought, and I allowed her one big hit to celebrate before she began her reduction cure. We went back to bed and fucked for a couple of hours, slowly and dreamily, and I forgot all about my worries of the night before.

• • •

I began to dole out progressively smaller amounts of gear to Cissy each morning, until after a week her habit had stabilised, and less than a quarter-gramme a day would keep her straight. I managed to resist the temptation to take another shot myself;

but after about ten days, while Cissy was out visiting a friend one afternoon, I chopped out a little line and sniffed it. I told myself that this was a much safer form of ingestion, and that anyway, ten days between doses of the drug was long enough for it to pass through my system — there would be no danger of my developing even a small habit from this. But I missed the rush, and thirty minutes later I found myself tying-off and locating the same vein in my left arm. Again, the shot nearly floored me, and the rush was so powerful this time that I had to run to the bathroom and throw up.

To someone who has never indulged, it must seem a mystery how anybody could possibly enjoy taking a drug that has this effect on the body (not to mention other potential dangers, such as overdose, hepatitis, HIV, and a whole host of minor infections, abscesses and possible damage to various bodily organs that go with the territory). All I can say is that the feeling is akin to being poised on top of a very high roller-coaster, staring down into the precipice and experiencing a mingled sensation of terror and excitement as the car accelerates and you feel your stomach fly up into your mouth — the main difference here being that seconds later you are in paradise. It's a feeling for nihilists and hedonists — for people who have either given up trying to make sense of existence, and want a quick and easy way out, or for people who don't give a shit about a future they can't see or believe in, and want only the most intense and immediate rush that life can offer.

Of course, in the beginning, you might just slide into it. Maybe someone offers you a chase at a party and you quite like the buzz you get off it; maybe you indulge a few times at a friend's house, and it's nothing particularly earth-shattering or special to you. But for those who have a genetic predisposition to smack (and the problem is, you don't know whether you have or not until you've tried it), such casual indulgence rapidly becomes an impossibility. Very quickly the drug takes over all areas and aspects of existence, until nothing else really matters except the rush, the warmth, and the freedom from anxiety that only heroin can bestow upon its legion of devotees.

I must have nodded out for a couple of hours, because suddenly Cissy was in the room, and she was not pleased.

"I knew this would happen, I just knew it! What, have you been using every day since you scored, or is this the first time? I thought you were supposed to be helping me, or was that just an excuse you were looking for? Jesus, now I've got this on my head as well — you gettin' back into gear — that's all I fuckin' need . . . shit!"

I didn't even bother trying to lie, or make excuses. The evidence was right there before me on the table: spoon, syringe, cotton, matches and gear, and although I knew I should feel humbled and apologetic, I felt myself getting angry instead.

"Look, it's only one time, for Christ's sake! I'm not gonna get back into it on a regular basis, am I? That'd be really stupid . . . an' anyway, you're not exactly in a position to be preaching."

"Yeah, but you're supposed to be helping me, you're supposed to be being strong. How am I gonna stop if I see that you're using all the time as well?"

I knew she was right, but at the same time I felt arrogant and without remorse — just angry at myself for getting caught.

"So, I fucked up, I admit it — I'm guilty as charged, if that makes you feel any better. Look, it's only twice, I'm not gonna get back into using every day, honest." As soon as the words were out of my befuddled brain, I felt like kicking myself.

"I thought you said it was the first time, you lyin' bastard! That probably means you've been using every day, smokin' or sniffin', if not actually shooting up — I bet you've got a fuckin' habit again already. Well, fuck off, if you're gonna get high then so am I, I'm sick of this tapering-off business — an' anyway, it's boring, an' I feel like you're controlling me. So come on, shit-head, give me a decent-sized hit . . . if you're gonna be high, I wanna get high too!"

I could hardly deny her under the circumstances, and I measured out a fairly large amount into the big silver spoon that lay on the table. I added water and lemon juice, and cooked the whole lot up until the hot brown liquid bubbled in the spoon, then drew half of it up into the syringe before handing it to Cissy. As she tied-off and tried to find a vein, I took another syringe and booted the rest of the freshly-cooked gear myself.

. . .

Within a week, I'd cultivated a nice little habit and was shooting up several times a day. I'd had to cop again almost immediately, the first quarter-ounce having largely disappeared, but I was able to score easily, and more this time, too. Cissy helped me to sell the stuff. She had numerous friends and contacts who were ready and willing to buy, mostly street junkie types who usually bought off the dealers that hung around the backstreets and alleys near King's Cross station, and a rapid turnover was essential if we were to support our own growing habits. I also bought an ounce of speed, as I knew many people who used the drug on a casual basis — just at weekends to go to concerts and parties — and it meant that if, for any reason, I couldn't manage to buy an amount of heroin, I would still have something to sell.

This meant that there was a constant stream of people in and out of the house at all hours of the night and day, and I was always worried that the neighbours would become suspicious and telephone the police. However, the fact that the squat was on a busy main road, full of pedestrians and traffic, and that there were other squats nearby, also with large and shifting populations, meant that our never-ending stream of visitors went largely unnoticed, or at least unheeded. I refused to do business after 9 p.m., unless it was a special favour to friends, but I was in a constant state of anxiety, always expecting the police to raid the place, especially as other people in the house were also dealing. A couple who had moved in downstairs were dealing hash — and speed also — and the boy who lived down the hallway from Andy's room sold acid; and although most of this drug activity was on a fairly low level, money-wise, it did mean there was a perpetual flow of variously weird and wasted people, arriving and leaving from early in the morning until late at night. Sometimes, the house resembled a non-stop drugs party with people coming and going at regular intervals, buying and consuming various drugs in the different rooms on each floor, often staying for hours at a time. It was not at all the discreet, anonymous premises of a professional drug dealer: loud music blared from each crazily decorated room, there were always bizarre scenes happening somewhere and the place was more like a mixture of commune and opium den than a serious money-making proposition.

My life, once again, fell into a routine of using and scoring, of hunting through the streets and council estates of North London and sitting in smokey, smelly rooms, often for hours on end, waiting for a delivery to arrive. At least I wasn't having to go out on a daily basis, though, only each week or ten days when stocks got low and had to be replenished, and the rest of the time I could sit up in our room getting high and waiting for customers to arrive. It beat working in the T-shirt factory, but I was also aware that a threshold had been crossed when I'd begun to use again. My relationship with Cissy was beginning to change, and it was no longer on the same basis that it had previously been. The bond which tied us together, now, was not so much love as a mutual need for the same drug: we became more jealous if one of us got high without the other than if either of us disappeared to spend the night with someone else.

Sometimes, I wouldn't be able to score, and both of us would be out tramping the streets, doing the round of small-time dealers who, like myself, sold individual wraps. We'd borrow and barter so that we wouldn't have to break into our float, hustling for a half or quarter-gramme, just to keep ourselves straight for a few hours, or until one of the main dealers was back in business. After just a few months, I'd accumulated an impressive cache of stolen goods — watches, CDs, radios, jewellery, clothes — received in lieu of payment for drugs, and these often came in handy at such times. One girl, Suzy, who used to buy speed off me and would consume amazing quantities of the stuff, was an especially good thief. She would turn up with the most unlikely objects — anything from a high-quality continental duvet to a complete set of bone china dinner-plates — and she would also steal to order: if you wanted a particular record, or CD, or a new pair of jeans, you would let her know, and she'd be back on the doorstep within a few hours, bringing the desired goods to be exchanged for a gramme or two of speed.

One of the characters I used to buy from, whenever I couldn't lay my hands on a large amount, was Bela, an Italian junkie who used to deal out of the public lavatories in Regent's Park. He had an English wife and a small child, and had recently secured himself a job with the local council, cleaning and maintaining the toilets at the Camden Town end of the park, next to London Zoo. He had a small office at the rear of the prefabricated building and would deal out of there, and on any particular day he would have anything up to two dozen junkies dotted around the grass and park benches, waiting to pay him a visit. It was an amusing sight to behold, all these pale, degenerate people sitting amongst the azalea and rhododendron bushes, pretending to be casually enjoying the watery spring sunshine while impatiently counting the minutes until it was their turn to meet the hallowed presence within. I don't know if

"Bela" was his real name — it could have been, or it might just have been a nickname derived from his thick, European accent; or from the fact that he so evidently enjoyed the act of shooting up in itself, booting and re-booting the blood time after time, as if fascinated by the sight, or the smell of it, and with an ash-laden cigarette dangling from one corner of his mouth throughout the whole procedure. Whatever the case, Bela was the most committed and unrepentant junkie I have ever met. He never thought of trying to straighten himself out, shouldering the burden of addiction as if it were his true calling in life, his one real interest, and about which he knew more than anyone else. His deals were lousy, but he never cut the gear, regarding this as sacrilege, so that while the quantity was always a little under, the quality was good. He justified these small deals by emphasising that, for him, the drug itself was like blood — his "lifeblood" he called it, with a toothless and maniacal grin — and that he needed it more than anybody else did. Sooner or later, most junkies come to believe this, and use it to justify their own greed; but with Bela heroin really was like a religion, and he its saint, or avatar. To watch him shooting up, especially if you were sick and impatient to cop, was like torture. In and out the blood would flow, as Bela booted the smack around his veins, and you couldn't interrupt or ask him to hurry — this would have been like urging haste on someone who was partaking of the holy sacrament. And so you would sit there, sweating and twitching, pretending you really weren't too concerned whether you scored or not — when in truth, every nerve and fibre of your body was screaming out for the precious elixir that was now being flaunted right before your eyes.

On several occasions I went with him to his house, and once he showed me his set of antique glass syringes, the type Sherlock Holmes would have used to inject himself with cocaine ("Purely for medicinal purposes, Watson"), and of which he was inordinately proud. He had a whole ritual for shooting up, and nothing could be allowed to interfere with this. In a room crowded with nappies, toys and drying laundry, and with the baby crying loudly for attention, he would carefully lay out the tools of his trade and prepare himself like a priest awaiting the presence of the Holy Spirit. Only afterwards, when he was satisfied that every last particle of the drug had been thoroughly absorbed into his bloodstream, could you talk to him again. The baby would be pacified, the room tidied, the dishes cleaned and life allowed to resume its normal flow — after which, finally, you would be allowed to score.

Eventually, of course, the Regent's Park shooting gallery was rumbled. A posse of police surrounded the lavatory building, just after Bela had bought half an ounce of new heroin and was busy in his office dividing it into smaller deals. Luckily, he had plenty of toilets to flush the stuff down, and with only a small amount of personal on him he got off with a six months suspended sentence. However, all his capital had gone, and the last time I saw him he was looking dirty and dishevelled, his clothes stank and he had been forced to sell his treasured set of glass syringes. He didn't seem too bothered, though, accepting this set-back philosophically as part of the price to be exacted in the service of his master, Lord Heroin. As he shuffled off to search for the next half or quarter-gramme, with the same toothless and insane grin, I noticed he had a big, spreading stain in the seat of his grimy, fawn-coloured trousers.

My main dealer, though, the person I bought quantity from, was Joe the Geordie. An archetypal Northern hard man, his place was like a fortress: he'd had a steel-reinforced double door fitted to his flat, and there were enough locks, keys and bolts to satisfy the warden of a maximum-security prison. Joe had been busted on several occasions in the past, and having done time inside was determined to avoid repeating the experience. Before he would allow me to buy from him, I had to meet him several times in various different pubs, so that he could check me out and satisfy himself that I wasn't part of some set-up, and on the first occasion he even shook me down to make sure that I wasn't carrying a wire for the police. After these pleasant and diverting formalities, I was finally accepted as being on the level and told the address to come to when I wanted to score. A telephone call had to be made first, though, and an elaborate but simplistic code followed, that would have fooled no-one listening in who was in possession of a more or less functioning brain — something along the lines of: "Hello, is Mr. Brown in please? Oh, he's not — could you tell me what time he'll be back, then?"; or, "Yes, I'd like to meet Mr. White, but I'd prefer it if Mr. Brown came along too"; or again, "A quarter past three would be okay, but half-past would suit me much better."

Joe had also had a video security camera installed above his front door, with a monitor in the bedroom, that gave him a perfect view of the hallway and whoever might be approaching, or lurking there. But even with all these precautions, the doorbell still had to be rung a certain number of times, and in a certain way, according to a code given over the phone before a visit ("two short, two long"), and which was changed each day. Without the correct code the door would not be opened, even if your face was known.

Once you had gained access to this castle-keep, you'd be confronted by a room full of other small-time dealers waiting to score. Joe would be in the bedroom dealing with one client at a time, painstakingly and precisely weighing out the heroin on a set of silver surgical scales while you'd take your place in the living-room queue, to be served mugs of coffee or tea by Joe's common-law wife, Jody. Both were from the North-East, both had been junkies for many years, and both had been inside on more than one occasion — I think they might even have been at school together. At any rate, they had a nice working relationship, and had managed to stay together through all the trials and tribulations that junkie life involves. Joe was my main connection for about six months and was always reliable, both in terms of quality and quantity. He never bought rubbish and passed it on to his clients, and if good stuff wasn't available he was straight up about it; then you would either have to take a chance and go elsewhere or wait until Joe had managed to score and was back in business again.

Finally, though, in spite of all his elaborate precautions, he was busted leaving the premises of a bigger dealer who the police had been watching for several weeks. He was carrying a couple of ounces shoved up his arse in a plastic bag; but a quick body-search back at headquarters soon revealed that, and he was sent down for four years, first to Brixton Prison, then later to some low-security joint in the Home Counties. Jody, true to form, stuck by him and would visit him regularly, passing small amounts of gear wrapped in silver foil, and hidden under her tongue, from her mouth to his when they kissed. This way, he was able to gradually taper off to minimise the pain and sickness of withdrawal.

After Joe, I had trouble finding a regular connection and was forced more and more to make do with second-rate stuff. Paradoxically, my own business was growing and an increasing number of people were visiting me, both for heroin and speed; but far from making me happy, this only heightened my paranoia. On some days, it seemed as if all the crazy, brain-damaged inhabitants of King's Cross and Camden Town were converging on us, and I was sure that by now we must be under police surveillance. But it was impossible to stop: I needed to maintain a rapid turnover of drugs and clients if our own ever-increasing habits were to be maintained, and I was forced to accept the risk that all these conspicuous characters brought with them, particularly as the house was a squat and not my own place. It seemed to act like a magnet for crazies of every shade, persuasion and description; but also for a never-ending stream of beautiful young girls, some of whom used, but many who didn't, often from good homes and wealthy families, who apparently came along to soak up the sleazy ambience — or something like that. The house, by now, had been painted in a variety of psychedelic, pornographic and gothic styles, depending on the drug and love-interests of the shifting population at any one time; the different coloured lights and art-work in each room, and on each floor, together with the clashing styles of music and noise that constantly blared from every doorway, gave you the feeling that you had wandered into the nightmare of some particularly disturbed mental patient. But it was home, and in spite of these occasional bouts of paranoia I felt more relaxed, and in a better frame of mind, than I ever had when living in Muswell hill and working at the T-shirt factory.

Sometime in the early summer, Cissy, Andy and I had a big bust-up. We had been lying together peaceably on the balcony at the rear of the house, looking down over the verdant and weed-choked back garden, enjoying the warm sunshine and drinking can after can of ice-cold beer. Andy had gone back inside to fetch another one, and was about to climb back out through the first-floor window, when Cissy made some remark, half jokingly, but with a sarcastic undertone. I don't remember exactly what she said, as I was drunk myself at the time, but whatever it was, Andy took immediate and extreme umbrage, hurling the opened beer can through the upper part of the window and showering Cissy and me with a mixture of broken glass and foaming beer. Though angry, I was befuddled and slow off the mark — but Cissy was through the window like a shot, chasing Andy into his room. By the time I arrived they were trading blows and screaming insults at each other.

"Arsehole! You could have blinded us with all that flying glass, you stupid twat!"

"Yeah, I'm an arsehole and you're a right fucking little bitch. Just keep your poisonous remarks to yourself in future!"

"Ah, piss off! You can't even take a joke anymore. You should learn how to laugh at yourself — everybody else does!"

All at once, Cissy upped the ante and began throwing Andy's possessions through the half-opened front window into the street: first cassettes, then records, then clothes, then the record-player — anything, in fact, that she could lay her hands on. At first, Andy stood back and allowed her to carry on unchecked, venting her rage; but then suddenly he rushed at her, pushing her so hard that she herself went hurtling towards the window, her head and shoulders crashing through the glass of the unopened upper section. Both Andy and I were shocked into momentary silence — I don't think he intended to actually push Cissy through the window — but then I went after him in a rage, getting him in a headlock and running his head repeatedly into one of the walls. All of us were drunk, and I was berserk with anger; but luckily, Jigg, one of the other temporary residents of the house, alerted by the shouts, screams, breaking glass and scattered possessions crashing onto the pavement outside his ground-floor window, rushed into the room and pulled me off Andy before I did him any serious damage. Miraculously, Cissy was unscathed and her face was not the cut and bleeding mask that I had expected. We all stood back panting, surveying the chaos around us in silence, then Cissy marched out of the room with her nose in the air and went upstairs. I followed, leaving Jigg with Andy to retrieve what was left of his possessions and to tidy up the mess. Cissy and Andy didn't speak to each other for a few days, but then they made up and it was as if the fight had never happened. Andy even gave her a mosaic, made from the broken pieces of glass and stuck onto a purple background, as a gift to commemorate the episode.

• • •

Towards midsummer, a group of about eight of us went up to the West Country for the Glastonbury Festival. I bought an old Bedford minibus off a friend for fifty pounds, and even though it was on its last legs I reckoned it would at least get us all there — we could worry about the return journey later. Of course, we took plenty of drugs with us: Rachel, a beautiful, red-haired, Pre-Raphaelite girl of about eighteen, who used to visit us a lot, had a few grammes of hash-oil secreted inside a condom and hidden in her vagina; Andy had about fifty hits of acid stashed under one of the seats; while I had speed and enough methadone to keep Cissy and me straight for the four or five days we would be at the festival. The van had a top speed of about 35 m.p.h., and was basically a heap of junk on wheels; so to avoid being stopped by the motorway police for going too slowly (we had no tax, or insurance either), and perhaps being searched for drugs, I took to the backroads and lanes, cruising between the hedgerows of the dreamy summer fields at a comfortable 30 m.p.h.

It took us about seven hours to cover the one hundred and twenty miles between London and Glastonbury, and it was early evening when we finally arrived. We'd decided to split the cost of one ticket between us, and that the rest of us would try to get in without paying and meet up later, so I drove around the lanes that circled the huge festival site, looking for a weak spot in the perimeter fence. Finally, in the headlights, I saw several people scrambling through a hole that someone had scraped in the earth beneath the high metal fence, and I dropped the others off to make their own way in. Then, I drove around to the main gate, paid my entrance fee, parked the van in one of the allotted fields and made my way to the pre-arranged meeting place to rendezvous with the others.

I don't remember a lot about the festival, and I certainly

don't remember seeing any bands. We pitched our tent in the Greenfield, amongst the "New Age" travellers, and spent most of the four days we were there wandering around in a chemical, drug-induced haze. The weather was scorching, and the members of some London-based art group had erected a huge "Car Henge" circle of wrecked automobiles, upended and placed on top of each other, dolmen-like, presumably in celebration of the coming end of mechanised civilisation. Cissy disappeared early on, and my main recollection is of fucking Rachel for most of the second night, after we had both taken speed and acid. Outside the tent, about a hundred drunk, stoned revellers beat out a crazy rhythm on the cars and metal sculptures, with sticks, stones, hammers, cans and bottles, as they welcomed the rising sun on midsummer's day.

When Cissy finally showed up on the fourth day, she was sick and in need of methadone, and as there was only a little left, we drank it together and decided to drive back to London that night. The others wanted to stay, but the thought of the stash of heroin waiting for us back at the squat, and the knowledge that by the following morning we would both be sick, was enough to dissuade us from doing likewise. And so, around dusk, we set off in the now seriously unreliable minibus, leaving our friends to make their own way back over the course of the next few days.

After about thirty miles, the headlights went off and refused to work again, and though I continued to drive along the white line in the middle of the road for awhile, the after-effects of the acid were playing havoc with my vision. I kept imagining shadows and shape-shifters jumping out of the darkened trees into our path, and coloured lights were still exploding behind my eyes. It was too dangerous, and after nearly running the van off the road a couple of times I decided to stop for the night, parking up some way along a deserted forest track. There, Cissy and I bedded down for the night in our sleeping bags, outside beneath the whispering, overarching trees.

My idea was to wake up with the sun, and drive the rest of the way to London before the methadone wore off and we began to get sick. However, I'd reckoned without the effects of four nights without sleep, and when we finally woke the sun was way past the zenith, and both of us were soaked in clammy, cold sweat inside our sleeping bags. Hurriedly, we gathered our things together and drove off at top speed, trying to ignore the chills, blurred vision and other manifestations of severe opiate depletion; but in our haste I pushed the van too hard, and as we hit the suburbs just west of Reading the engine finally seized, the vehicle coasting to a stop after a series of shuddering jolts.

"Oh that's just great! Now we're marooned out here in the wilderness, sick an' dirty, an' with no way of gettin' back home. Trust you to buy an old wreck that's ready for the knacker's yard."

"Oh sod off, at least it got us there, didn't it? What d'you expect for fifty quid, anyway?!"

Fighting back the nausea, and with the sweat pouring off me, I stuck my head under the bonnet, even though I knew it would be a waste of time. With my rudimentary knowledge of mechanics, and judging by the sound the expiring engine had made, I was pretty sure that the big end had gone and that the van was now fucked beyond repair. I managed to get it into a side-street, where we abandoned it, carrying our things and hitch-hiking the remaining forty or fifty miles back to London. By the time we arrived in Camden Town, we were both suffering severe withdrawal symptoms, and Cissy was undergoing some kind of paroxysm of self-loathing over our unwashed, rancid state. The first thing we did on arriving home was to cook up a huge shot of heroin, which we shared, before falling into a deep, untroubled sleep that lasted until the afternoon of the following day.

• • •

Shortly after returning from this jaunt, Cissy and I both had accidents that laid us up in bed for several weeks. We had been to visit friends, and were returning to the squat on one of the old "Routemaster" buses — the type with a conductor and an open rear door — and were approaching our stop when Cissy decided that she would jump off while the bus was still in motion. She misjudged the distance to the pavement and badly twisted her ankle against the concrete kerbstone, sprawling full-length and scraping her face into the bargain. By the time I reached her, she was jumping up and down on one foot, yelling at the top of her voice.

"Ow, ow, ow, Jesus fuckin' Christ, I've busted it! Don't just stand there, do something, get me inside for fuck's sake — hurry up babe, please, it's killin' me!"

Even before I got her indoors, her ankle had swollen to twice its normal size, and in spite of ice-packs and cold water compresses, it refused to go down. I took her to UCH in Euston, and after several hours wait she finally emerged from the casualty department with a walking-stick and a bandage up to her knee.

"Well, at least it's not broken . . ."

"That's alright for you to say, but a torn tendon's almost as bad — it hurts like fuck, an' I'm not supposed to put any weight on it for the next six weeks. Basically, it means I'm gonna be laid up for the rest of the summer — I'm gonna go mad cooped up in the room in this heat . . . An' what about Rosie, who'll take her for walks? I'm gonna be reliant on you for everything — drugs, food, cigarettes, everything, which is just bloody great! Well, you always did want to control me, so now you've got your wish!"

By the time we reached home, her bad temper and paranoia had subsided, and I propped her up in bed with plenty of pillows so that she could rest her leg. As soon as she was settled, I gave her a big shot of smack to alleviate the pain.

Then, the very next day, while I was fixing a clogged drainpipe at the rear of the house, I fell off the rickety old stepladder I was using and crashed twelve or fifteen feet onto the concrete patio below. The pipe had backed up and over-flowed, leaving a pool of foul-smelling, putrefying water directly outside the back door, and as no-one else seemed to give a fuck, I had foolishly taken it upon myself to repair it. As I balanced precariously on top of the ladder, Purley Pete, one of the other occupants of the squat, shouted up instructions from below:

"Try it from the elbow-bend first — that's the most likely place for it to have got blocked, and you can see what's hap-penin' if you take the collar off the join an' stick your 'and inside."

I undid the screws which clamped the two sections of pipe together, and pulled them carefully apart — nothing.

"That's odd — it must be blocked further up, in the straight section, which is pretty unusual. Try tappin' it with an 'ammer, you should be able to tell from the sound which bit is full of water."

I was now on the very top step of the ladder, and the only way I could go any higher was to place my right foot on one of the stays which clamped the pipe to the edge of the house. I tapped it gently with the hammer, up and down, and listened carefully for any change of tone. And it was true: at a point just about level with the top of my head, I was pretty sure I could detect a distinct difference in the way the pipe sounded — much denser, as if there were something solid inside.

"The only way to get in from there is to crack it open, then repair it later. There's no collar further up, so that's all you can do, really . . ."

Luckily, the pipe was of the old-fashioned, heavy-duty porcelain variety, and I was easily able to crack a hole in it with a few well-aimed hammer blows. I reached inside, and about three inches above my eye-level I finally located the blockage. It appeared to be some kind of jagged metal, but soft and easily manipulated, the kind of metal they use in — Yes! — beer cans!

"Some daft cunt's dropped a can of Special Brew down inside the pipe. It must have been that party we had last month — some mates of Andy's got out through the attic, and were sittin' around on the roof, drinkin' and smokin'. It must have been one of them did it for a laugh, dropped it down from where the guttering feeds into the pipe — fuckin' typical!"

I poked at the can with a screwdriver, trying to dislodge it, but it was wedged firmly inside the pipe. Finally, I managed to get a proper grip on it and yanked hard, so that the offending can of Special Brew, twisted and torn, was now more than halfway out of the hole.

"Watch out for the water when you pull it through . . ."

"Yeah, yeah!"

I gave the can one final hard tug, taking care not to lose my balance, or my grip on the pipe . . .

"Jesus Christ! Shit!"

I jumped backwards off the ladder, twisting away in mid-air, as a huge, black water-snake shot out of the hole and came spiralling straight towards my face. It had obviously hatched in the pipe and, having been trapped there, had grown bigger and bigger until I'd unwittingly released it by breaking the pipe open and giving it an escape route. I didn't know if it was poisonous, or not; but the thought of its slimy, black body propelling itself directly at my throat was enough — I wasn't going to stick around to find out, and I instinctively dived backwards off the ladder to escape its spitting, snarling jaws.

I hit the ground hard, heels first, and as the pain shot up my legs and through my body, I cried out loud in agony. But I was also laughing like a fool, as I'd realised my mistake even before I hit the ground: what I had tried to get away from was not a water-snake at all, just oozing, black mud, forced out of the hole at great speed by the pressure of the water trapped above. But now the pain was excruciating. Stupidly, I had undertaken the task wearing only soft-bottomed karate slippers on my feet, and although I'd managed to land squarely, they provided no protection at all against the impact. I tried to ignore the pain, hoping it would go away, and sat outside in the late-afternoon sun with both feet plunged in a bucket filled with ice-cold water; but when, after about an hour, I attempted to stand, I could put no weight at all on either foot and immediately fell over. Pete helped me into a taxi, and for the second time in two days I found myself in the casualty department of UCH. When I was finally attended to, and x-rays had been taken, I was told that I had fractured the heel bone of each foot; and, furthermore, that this was probably the worst bone to break in the entire human body, as a cast could not be put on it. Once fractured, it was always liable to break again if a similar accident occurred at any time in the future.

Buoyed up by this heartening news, and equipped with a pair of crutches and a set of heel-pads, I was told to report back in three weeks for a check-up and further x-rays, then carried to a waiting taxi by Pete and a hospital orderly. I was also assured that it would be at least eight weeks before I could even think of putting any weight on my heels, and that I should spend as much of this time as possible in bed, arranging for someone else to do all my errands and running around for me. I got no sympathy at all from Cissy.

"You dickhead — why'd you decide to wear slippers to fix the drains? Anyone with any sense at all would have worn work-boots . . . An' it's a wonder, anyway, that old stepladder didn't give way beneath you. You could have broken your neck, not just your heels. Fuckin' water-snake . . . !"

"Yeah, it's almost as clever as jumping off moving buses with your eyes closed . . ."

"Oh belt up, that could have happened to anyone!"

As we lay side by side, both of us propped up on pillows on Cissy's queen-sized bed, I looked forward to spending the next few weeks like this, immobilised and unable to escape from each other, and to all the bickering and bitching that this confinement was bound to engender. But of course, the thought that was uppermost in my mind was: "How the fuck am I gonna be able to cop and keep dealing in this state, and who can I trust to help me out?"

● ● ●

Somerstown Sammy was a friend of Cissy's, a rat-faced little street junkie with a speech impediment and an ingratiating manner that annoyed the hell out of me. Also known as "Whisper", because of the virtually sub-audible way in which he spoke, he was basically one of her disciples, and was content to worship her from afar whenever he came around to score. He had pale, grey eyes, and his blotchy, freckled skin was drawn tight across the bones of his face, so that in certain lights, and from certain angles, he seemed to be translucent, as if the light passed right through him. His personality, too, was somehow vaporous and ill-defined, so that if I tried to recall his appearance in detail, or his manner, when he was not actually sitting in the room right there in front of me, I found that I could not. He had a thin, wispy beard, pointed and flecked with grey, which he nervously tugged at whenever he spoke, and he always wore grey, even in the summer: a grey bomber jacket and flannel trousers when it was hot; a long, grey overcoat when it was cold. He was able to make himself invisible in a crowd, to pass amongst people unseen and unheeded, and because of this talent he was an expert thief. Quite simply, people just didn't notice him, and he was able to glide up and down the aisles of large department stores unmolested by detectives and security guards, slipping valuable objects into the specially-sewn linings of his jackets and coats. Vapid and diminutive as he was, he would be out of the door and onto the street again before his presence had even registered in the consciousness of those employed to watch.

Knowing him like this, I was dubious, to put it mildly, when Cissy came up with the idea of asking him to score for us while we were laid up in bed. I didn't trust or particularly like Sammy, and while it was true that, in terms of his knowledge of the network of heroin dealers around King's Cross and Camden, he was probably the most qualified of our acquaintances, I was also aware of the dangers of placing all our capital in the hands of such a shifty character. Cissy was convinced he was the man for the job, though, and used all her powers of persuasion to get me to agree.

"Really, babe, he's okay, believe me, an' he knows the scene better than anyone else — he's been around for years, an' he won't buy shit or anything that's cut too bad. An' you know how he worships me — he wouldn't dream of rippin' us off."

"I don't know . . . I just don't like the idea of giving all our money to somebody who basically makes a living from thievin', even if he is a friend of yours. It's too dangerous — if anything goes wrong, we're gonna be up Shit Creek without a paddle . . . no money, no gear, and both of us laid up like cripples in bed."

"What's the alternative? Can you think of anyone else who knows so many dealers, and who the dealers would trust to sell to? I can't, I'm sure. Come on, the guy's in love with me, he'll do anything I ask, I've got him like this around my little finger — an' he wouldn't dare rip us off, in case I don't let him visit us anymore."

Cissy appeared intent on making the situation into some kind of demonstration of her feminine power and hold over a helpless male admirer; but, at the same time, it was true that

Sammy did know the heroin scene better than anyone else I could think of. Within a few days we would be out of smack again, and I needed to score soon; as it was impossible for me to hunt through the streets and estates on broken feet, it was essential to find someone who would do the running around for me. I didn't like the idea, but Sammy did seem to be the only person with the qualifications necessary for the job, so I decided to trust Cissy's instincts and go along with her plan. But it was with severe misgivings that I watched him walk out of the door a few days later with over nine hundred pounds of my float in his pocket.

As the hours passed, the sinking feeling in my stomach became ever more pronounced, and though at first Cissy was dismissive, telling me to stop worrying and relax, as night drew in and Sammy had still not returned, she too began to worry and became silent and withdrawn. Finally, at around 11:30, the doorbell rang and someone downstairs let Sammy in. But I knew before he entered the room that the deal had gone wrong — his footsteps were slow and reluctant as he climbed the stairs, not at all the tread of someone who has just successfully scored a large amount of heroin and is now looking forward to sampling the goods.

"I got taken off, man, r-r-r-really, I'm s-s-sorry, but it was a rip-off — the guy disappeared with your money and n-n-never came back," Sammy whispered and stammered from where he stood in the doorway.

"Who did? You mean to say you . . . ? Why'd the fuck you give it to someone to go off with anyway?!" Cissy screamed before I had a chance to say anything. "I thought you were going to Frank's to score, or if not then to Angie's place. Why'd you give the money to somebody else, for Christ's sake?!"

"F-F-Frank was away, and Angie only had a little bit, so I went up to D-D-D-Dodgy Dave's — I've scored off him before, and he's always been straight with me. But he didn't have anything either, there's a real drought at the moment, l-l-lots of b-busts and people are laying low. But there was this one guy at Dave's, claimed to know where to s-score, but he had to go alone — I mean I wasn't happy either, but Dave told me he was okay, and I was gettin' desperate. I'm f-f-f-fuckin' sick as well, you know, and it was either that, or nothin'. Look, I'm s-sorry, but maybe he'll show up tomorrow — I mean Dave's pissed off as well, he's a mate of his, and sooner or later he'll track him down, he's b-b-bound to . . ."

"What, you gave all our money to some total fucking stranger, and just let him walk off with it? Are you crazy?!" I just couldn't believe that Sammy had been so stupid. In fact, I didn't believe him at all. His story was just about plausible, but he was an old hand at this game and shouldn't have been taken in so easily, even allowing for his desperation and growing dope-sickness. "I think you're full of shit — you've stashed the money somewhere, and you're just covering your own tracks by coming back here with this bullshit story. You'll leave here, and the first thing you'll do is go back home and get high while me an' Cissy'll be stuck here without money, or gear."

"N-n-n-no way, I wouldn't do that, you two are my friends, and I w-w-wouldn't do something so shitty to people I c-c-care about! Look, you can check my story with D-Dodgy Dave if you don't believe me, he'll back me up in everything I s-s-say." Sammy was almost in tears at this point — sweat was breaking out on his forehead, and he was shaking and trembling all over. He was obviously starting to withdraw, but I refused to believe that anyone with as much experience of the scene as he had could have been fooled so easily. If there is one cardinal rule to follow when copping, it's never give your money to strangers, even if you are sick and desperate and they promise you the earth. Or, if you do, go with them and don't let them out of your sight for a minute, even to go to the toilet — otherwise, they'll be out of the window and around the corner before you know it, and you'll be left high and dry, feeling like the idiot you truly are for trusting them in the first place.

Cissy had fallen silent during my tirade; but suddenly she spoke up from the shadows in the corner of the room, where she was sitting with her knees drawn up to her chin, watching us intently.

"Aw, leave him alone, he's tellin' the truth, can't you see? It's too late, the money's gone, an' shoutin' at Sammy ain't gonna bring it back, is it? Yeah, he was stupid, but look, he's sick as a dog. C'mon Sammy, I've got a bit of gear stashed for emergencies, enough to keep us all straight until the morning, anyway."

I stared at her in amazement. Usually, she was acquisitive and possessive as far as smack was concerned, and I couldn't believe she was offering our last little bit to someone I still suspected of rippng us off. I felt more like strangling the cunt than getting high with him, but it was true what Cissy said — one way or another the money was gone, and all the yelling and shouting in the world wasn't going to bring it back. Anyway, I was starting to believe Sammy's story — if he had stolen the money himself, he could easily have disappeared with no fear of my coming after him, laid up as I was, and there was nothing to be gained for him by returning to us and telling a pack of lies. I began to see him as the pathetic, lost soul he truly was, realising that Cissy and I were probably the best friends he had — or at least that was how he saw us. As I injected myself with the last of the gear, I cursed Sammy's stupidity and my own bad luck; but most of all I cursed my idiocy for trusting Cissy's judgement, for allowing myself to get back into the situation of no money, no smack and not just one enormous habit to feed each day, but two.

• • •

I always used to keep a few hundred milligrammes of methadone hidden under the floorboards of our room, in case of busts or general heroin shortages, and I figured this would be enough to keep us straight, at least for a week or so. Once this ran out, though, I had no idea where I was going to get enough capital together to start dealing again. It had taken me over a year working at the factory to save just the small amount of money I had begun with, and I had no rich parents or fairy godmothers to fall back upon. So when Cissy suggested using the money that Julia had lent her months before, supposedly to start a club with, I wasn't exactly reluctant to go along with the idea. I had forgotten all about this loan, and though it meant that Cissy would now be in control of the money supply, I didn't foresee any particular problems with this: I had shared everything with her, treating her as an equal partner, and I expected that she would now do the same with me. For her part, Cissy was worried in case Julia suddenly asked her to return the money, or got wind that she had spent it all on drugs. But as they had not seen each other for a couple of months now, and as Julia was a rich bitch and not exactly hard up for cash, I managed to calm her fears, persuading her that she could always pay the money back in installments in the unlikely event that the loan was suddenly called in.

After about ten days, the constant throbbing in my heels had subsided a little, and I had taught myself how to get around quite effectively by swinging between the two crutches, landing on the toes of both feet together so that my heels never had to touch the ground. I could project myself forward quite rapidly like this, and soon I was hurtling around the streets and council estates as quickly as if the accident had never happened. Life returned to its normal pattern of scoring, dealing and getting high and, as my business grew, I was able to increase the amount I was buying each time from a half to three quarters of an ounce — not exactly big-time dealing, but enough to ensure that we could survive quite comfortably, both in terms of the drugs we needed and for everyday necessities such as food and travel. We didn't lead much of a social life anyway. Everything revolved around the squat, our friends were the people who bought from us and it was always they who visited, rarely vice-versa. My happiest times were when I was returning from scoring, a small plastic bag of junk stuffed inside my pants, and the anticipation of sampling this new batch uppermost in my mind as I climbed the shadowy stairways of our house. I rarely thought about the future, not in terms of plans and ambitions anyhow. As long as I had enough smack to last a week or ten days ahead, that was enough for me, while the thought of a nice little stash hidden away beneath the floorboards filled me with a warm, rosy glow — I felt safe, secure and at ease with life.

Such apathy towards the future is common enough amongst junkies — it is, after all, one of the most dead-end forms of existence you could hope to choose — and on the rare occasions that I did think about it, I realised that, for me, it was so out of reach, so beyond my ability to control or influence, that it really didn't seem worth the effort. Easier, by far, just to take another shot and wallow in the slough of negativity and self-obliteration that is the natural element of the long-term user. In fact, I took such a perverse pleasure in not having a future that I elevated it to the position of a philosophy, some kind of code to live by, which fully satisfied all my deepest and most intense antisocial tendencies. For the act of shooting smack is like a one-fingered salute to society, a rejection of all the values we are taught to revere, respect and admire: patience; hard work; self-denial; the postponement of pleasure as a reward for labour; in other words, the whole Puritan ethic. And I felt more in tune with criminals and sociopaths than I ever did with the worker who finds his niche in the system and, by all his effort and striving, only helps to perpetuate the machine that is strangling us all. Never mind that I was destroying myself in the process. This, too, afforded me a grim pleasure; and whenever I temporarily stopped using, and felt my natural energies returning, I would feel compelled to dissipate and obliterate them by a quick return to junkiedom, so thoroughly uncomfortable did this sensation make me feel. I distrusted all manifestations of so-called natural love and affection, and the relationships I chose were always based more on strategies of mental and emotional abuse than upon what is usually understood by the word "love". Unless the person I was with was causing me intense pain, I simply wasn't happy, and I actively sought out relationships that were hopeless, doomed, fucked-up and twisted.

My most treasured moments were those I spent alone, though, or in the company of a few like-minded friends, gouched-out and oblivious with the smack coursing through my veins. I didn't care that Cissy and I were growing further apart, or that my original reason for starting to deal — namely, to get her away from junk — had disappeared along the way. I was too fucked-up myself, now, to give much thought to anything apart from dealing and scoring, and I was shooting either speed or smack from the moment I woke in the early afternoon until I eventually crashed out, usually around dawn.

• • •

"Push harder, for fuck's sake, can't you?!"

I was sick and perched on the edge of my chair, and as my guts went into spasm I fought to keep down the rising tide of vomit that threatened to engulf me at any moment. Ten days without a decent hit, and now this . . .

"Shut up, for Christ's sake, you sound like a fuckin'

midwife. You're puttin' me off, an' it's just goin' deeper inside."

Dodgy Dave was crouched in the middle of the floor, his pants around his ankles and an old copy of *The Sun* spread out beneath him. After one of the longest droughts in living memory, that had seen all the local dealers out desperately tramping the streets, Dave had finally managed to score a few grammes. The only problem was that he'd suffered an attack of the jitters and had hidden it so far up his own arse that he was now having severe problems finding it again.

"Look, it must be in there somewhere, it can't have disappeared completely. Can't you locate it with your fingers?"

"That's alright for you to say, you callous cunt . . . I've 'ad the shits for a week and me arse is like a baboon's. I could get me whole fist up there, and still not find it!"

Normally, I'd have had enough methadone to see me through times like this, but Cissy and I had had another of our increasingly frequent rows, and she'd disappeared with three hundred mls. of 'done and about half our float. Never mind that it was, in theory, her money — I couldn't believe her treachery, and I was ready to kill her when she eventually showed up.

"Maybe you should have a rest for a few minutes, take a cigarette break, then try again. Your muscles are obviously spasming an' going into reverse, so if you just relax for awhile they'll start working normally again, an' the bag'll come out by itself." Dave had the reputation of being a bit of a hard case, and I didn't want to get him riled.

"How the fuck can I relax with you sittin' there like a cunt, an' me bollock-naked with three grammes of smack up me arse. I'm sicker than you are, at least you 'ad a little bit to keep you goin' for awhile."

The spider's web tattoo that covered the right side of Dave's neck was throbbing with indignation, or maybe with the effort of trying to force out the stubborn little package that had lodged itself somewhere in the lower reaches of his small intestine. He used to shoot up in the middle of this tattoo, right in the jugular, when he couldn't raise a vein in his arms, hands or feet, and reckoned it gave him a better, faster rush than anywhere else.

"Why'd you stick it up your arse anyway? Couldn't you just have put it in your sock, or down your pants, like any normal person? I mean, if the Ol' Bill were onto you an' took you down the nick that's the first place they'd look."

I was reaching a crisis point of anxiety and impatience, and I thought for a moment that I might have pushed Dave too far. With no endorphins left in my system to cushion the pain, and no smack either, each movement was an effort — my bones grated in their sockets, my diaphragm pressed in upon my lungs and every nerve in my body was irritated and tortured to the point where I felt like screaming. But I also knew I had to tread carefully. Even though it was my money he had used to cop with, Dave was in no mood to be pressured or hustled. As he said, he was probably even sicker than I was, and though we had both been out hunting all day, with the sweat pouring off us and our skins crawling with the chills of withdrawal, it was he who had been successful and had eventually managed to score. He stood up looking very pissed-off, and for a minute I thought he might walk out on me with the smack still up his arse; but suddenly, his expression changed.

" 'ang on a minute — I felt somethin' move inside me, I think it's comin' out! Standin' up just then must've dislodged it, or else me guts're startin' to work again. Tha's funny, I didn't think there was anything left up there to shit out . . ."

Dave hopped back to his copy of *The Sun* and squatted down again. Puffing and grunting, with his face almost purple from the effort, he suddenly let out an almighty fart, and with it a horrible, stinking mess of watery diarrhoea spattered onto the newspaper. The stench was truly disgusting, but this timely and heaven-sent bowel movement had done the trick. Wiping his backside on a rancid old towel that was lying around, and with his face contorted in pain, Dave probed and prodded until his questing fingers finally locked around the elusive little package that had caused him so much anguish.

"Fuckin' A! Party time at last!"

He held the small, round bag aloft in victory. It was tightly wrapped in cling film and, as far as I could tell, had not been impregnated by the foul-smelling discharge. Dave was rumoured to be HIV positive, and I wasn't too happy about the gear having been stuffed up his backside in the first place; but as far as I knew, the virus could only be passed via blood or semen and was not able to travel through plastic, even when the plastic had been wedged far inside the carrier's arsehole.

Besides, Dave had already cleaned and sliced open the package with a razor blade, and was carefully measuring out a shot into his spoon; and with the stuff right there on the table in front of me, and with cold, sickly sweat breaking out from every pore in my body, I was willing to take my chances. I'd been sharing needles and having unprotected sex for years, both in New York and London, long before anyone knew anything about AIDS, and when it was still referred to as "Gay Cancer." Though the frequent TV warnings and documentaries were making me increasingly paranoid, I reckoned that this was a fairly safe bet, compared to the multifarious ways I'd already abused my body over the previous ten years.

The sense of anticipation a sick junkie feels as he cooks up his shot is almost impossible to describe. Maybe it is comparable to the sensation a man dying of thirst in the desert feels as he crawls up that final sand dune and unexpectedly sees water shimmering in the distance, a cool and welcoming oasis; or to the way a convict on Death Row might feel, suddenly and inexplicably pardoned and transported to a hotel room where the most beautiful and sexually-adept whore in the world waits to satisfy his every perverse fantasy and need. But not really.

To the person who has never been in this state, no words can truly convey the sense of expectation, the knowledge that within seconds all the pain and physical suffering will magically evaporate, like a dank river mist at sunrise. Your body, taken off the rack at last, will find itself instead floating in warm and protective amniotic waters, while your mind, tortured for days by darkness, gloom and ugly, twisted dreams, will suddenly be immune and inviolate, free from all anxiety and violent self-loathing. Artificial paradise it may well be; but in another sense, it is as real as real gets.

As I cooked up my own shot, my trembling hands became sure and precise, and I heated the spoon from below without spilling a drop. My clothes and body stank, and I was aware of the rancid discharge from my cock that was soiling the inside of my underwear. For when you are kicking, the genitals become hyper-sensitive and you tend to shoot off spontaneously, without warning, just from the pressure of your clothes against your skin. Even the air itself seems to hurt: you truly cannot stand any kind of contact upon your body at all, while friction of even the slightest and most innocuous kind is enough to send you into a shivering, quivering mass of jangled nerve endings and twitching flesh, as if plagues of insects were crawling about under your cold, clammy skin.

But all these symptoms vanish once the smack is in your veins, and you are suddenly flooded with a holy and trans-forming inner light. The decaying, stinking carcass that you have been forced to inhabit for days is suddenly charged with a marvellous energy, and you are awash with optimism, ideas and vague but pleasant dreams for the future. You wash the stench from your body and clothes, while the poisonous, cloy-ing dredge in your mind is flushed out, purified by the brief alchemical glow that is King Heroin's gift to even his most abject disciples.

I stuck the needle in, drew up the blood, booted it and

repeated the procedure, before following Dave into the Land of Nod, the smack-head's reward for all the pain, suffering and humiliation that is an essential part of his chosen way of life. For several hours I passed in and out of dreams, losing all sense of place and time, and when I finally came to Dave was gone. So, I duly noticed, was most of the remaining gear. He'd obviously felt that his traumatised anus entitled him to an extra gramme or two and had helped himself, probably feeling perfectly justified in doing so; and though I briefly flirted with the idea of taking a baseball bat and going to look for the cunt, I soon shelved it. I figured he was much harder than me, and anyway, by the time I found him the smack would be long gone. Instead, I cooked up what was left of the gear and shot it into my arm, recognising as I did so that whichever way I looked at the situation it was now impossible to deny that I was well and truly fucked.

· · ·

It was a dark night in early winter when I first ran into him, one of those typical London nights where a damp, lowering sky seems to absorb all the neon and electricity of the city, reflecting it back dully in a sick and oppressive orange glow. A fine, but cold, drizzle slanted across the street lamps and was gradually soaking through my outer layers of clothing, while the sock on my right foot was sodden and freezing from the water that leaked in through the hole in my shoe. I'd not seen Cissy for over three weeks now, and my anger at her for disappearing with the money and methadone had long since turned to worry. I'd searched all over for her, visiting the friends and acquaintances I knew she had around the North London drug scene, then trying further afield, in Brixton and Stockwell — but apparently no-one had seen or heard anything of her. I'd called Julia in Kensington, the place where Cissy usually went whenever she wanted to disappear, but if Julia knew anything of her whereabouts, she certainly wasn't letting on. I began to imagine all the situations and predicaments she might have got herself into — for if she had been dealing, I would have heard about it, and if she wasn't, then the methadone and money would have run out by now. First, I reckoned, she would have bought as much smack as she could possibly lay her hands on; then, when that ran out, instead of holding onto the methadone she would have sold it on the street to buy more gear. I believed I knew her ways, and that as long as there was any chance at all of getting hold of some skag she would take it, even though the methadone would keep her straight for much longer. The more I thought about it, the more I felt sure that Julia was telling the truth about not having seen her. After all, we had blown most of the money that Cissy had been fronted, and she would be unwilling to put herself in a position where she might have to admit this to someone she looked up to and regarded as her benefactress and protector.

I turned the possibilities over in my mind. Perhaps she had met someone else, someone from outside the drug scene who could give her the support she needed to kick the habit and had moved in with him. Our last row had been pretty nasty, and she'd stormed off into the night after telling me to "Fuck off and die"; but it was no worse, really, than any of the other arguments we'd been having of late, and anyway, where would she have met such a character? All our movements were connected with drugs, and with the people who used them, and since I'd been dealing she hadn't needed to work, or to move in circles where she might have met someone from outside the scene.

Again, if she had moved in with another dealer, or with someone else who used, I would have heard about it through the grapevine, and so far all my enquiries had drawn a blank: she seemed to have vanished into the air. No-one I knew had heard anything about her, nobody had seen her, and this gave rise to my greatest fear, one which I tried to keep at bay, but which constantly haunted me. As I twisted and turned in my sweat-soaked bed during the sleepless and feverish nights that seemed to go on forever, I saw visions of Cissy overdosed in a room somewhere, amongst people who didn't care, one way or the other, about the wasted little junkie girl slumped in the corner — except, maybe, as an inconvenience, a piece of human wreckage that somehow had to be disposed of. I tried to keep this image out of my mind, to think of some other explanation for her disappearance, but it kept on returning to haunt me. In my mind's eye, I would see her body dumped in some obscure place — disused industrial land, or amongst the weeds at the edge of some river or canal — destined to be just another statistic on police files when she finally was discovered.

I telephoned all the London hospitals, but no-one answering to Cissy's description had been brought in. I drew the same result when I checked with the police to see if she had been busted or arrested for some other offence. Pushing the most negative possibility from my mind, I tried to think rationally — where would a girl who needed at least fifty pounds each day in ready cash go to get it? I went down to Soho and traipsed around the clip-joints and peep-shows, talking to the girls in the pay-booths and the hawkers on the streets, with an old photo of Cissy from the time when she had short hair. I'd worked in one of these places myself, years before, when I first moved down to London, and I knew how cagey people were about giving out information. Consequently, I wasn't exactly surprised when I again drew a blank. Another, less attractive, possibility was the red-light district in the backstreets behind King's Cross station, a place where the most fucked-up and hopeless street whores in London worked, and where only punters in need of a serious sleaze fix went. It was while I was making my way towards this area one night that I first set eyes on him.

I don't know what made me take a detour to the street where Cissy's old flat was, or even less, what possessed me to climb the stairs of the tenement building that she used to live in. Somehow, my feet seemed to walk there of their own accord. Maybe it was sentiment that took me there; or maybe I hoped that by visiting this scene of former good times I would pick up some psychic current that would eventually lead me to her. Whatever the case, as I climbed the dimly-lit stairway I could hear the sound of someone else's footsteps ahead of me, echoing off the concrete flagstones and the old porcelain wall tiles, maybe two or three landings higher. Cissy's old apartment was on the fourth floor of the five-storey building, and I was sweating and breathless from the constant state of semi-withdrawal that I always seemed to be in these days.

Suddenly, up above me, these other footsteps halted, and I heard three sharp knocks on a wooden door, the sound echoing and reverberating around the concrete and steel of the dingy stairwell. It seemed that no-one was in, as the same knock was repeated once more, and I could hear the sound of pacing feet, as if the person was angry or frustrated at finding the flat empty and was not sure whether to try again or to leave. By now, I was approaching the third floor landing, and it was obvious that the person ahead of me was trying to gain access, either to Cissy's old flat or the one directly opposite. I heard a boot crash against the wood of the door — one, two, three times — and the sound of muttered cursing as the lock refused to yield; then, as I rounded the final bend in the stairs and reached the fourth floor, the burly figure in the dark blue padded anorak turned, and our eyes locked. I knew him immediately, and instinctively, even before I saw the old battle-scar down the left side of his face. But what was even stranger — and even more disturbing — was that he seemed to know me. Not a word was spoken as I passed by him and continued on up to the fifth floor, as if there was someone on this landing that I had come to visit; but something flashed between us, some kind of unconscious recognition, and I knew in that same moment why Cissy had disappeared: Scottish Dougie was out of prison and back in London, either for the purposes of revenge, or to reclaim what he believed to be his.

• • •

To make it convincing, I chose one of the two doors on the top landing and knocked loudly on the wood panelling, hoping that there would be no-one inside. If there was, I would quickly have to invent some bullshit story about a non-existent person, or a mistaken address I'd been given; but luckily, no-one came to answer the door, so I knocked again, even more loudly this time, to make it doubly convincing. Dougie was still lurking about on the floor below, and I was hoping he would leave ahead of me as I didn't want the fucker following me down the stairs and out onto the street. I was sure that somehow he had intuitively sussed the connection between Cissy and myself (how, I didn't know, but I definitely felt it), and I didn't want him following me home with the mistaken idea that I would lead him to her. He didn't budge, though, and I had to pass by him again on my way down the stairs. Again, no words were spoken, but I felt his eyes burning into the back of my head as I descended, and when I reached the second-floor landing I heard his footsteps start to follow, as if he had suddenly decided that I was, indeed, the lead he had been looking for. I took care not to increase my pace; but as soon as I was out of the tenement entrance, I sprinted along the street and ducked down the first alleyway I came to before Dougie had emerged from the building.

I knew the area well, and after criss-crossing a few more backstreets and alleys I felt sure that I had shaken him off, quickly making my way back to the squat. There, I cooked up a few old cottons to steady my nerves and take the edge off the sweating and the sickness that had suddenly returned with a vengeance. I'd managed to score a couple of grammes with the little money I still had left after Dodgy Dave had ripped me off, but this had soon gone and I'd been hustling ever since — calling in favours and exchanging the stolen goods I still possessed for the odd quarter or half-gramme wrap. I'd never ripped any of my customers off, or pulled power trips on them, and had often advanced them gear when they didn't have the readies to pay up-front; but I soon found out that this didn't mean such behaviour would necessarily be reciprocated. People I'd helped out when they were sick and desperate, and who were now dealing, conveniently forgot about their own past misfortunes, telling me how impossible it was for them to give me credit — no money, no gear — even though they would have loved to do so, if only the circumstances had been different. Not everyone was like this — a few dealers helped me out by fronting me small amounts — but I made a mental note of those who wouldn't, or who tried to make me crawl, and I made up my mind that if I ever got the chance in the future I would fuck these bastards over, one way or another.

As soon as I'd calmed down, I began to think. I felt sure, now, that Cissy was alive and well, and had gone to ground when she discovered that Dougie was out of jail and on the prowl in London. She would be scared for herself — possibly for me also — and though I still had no idea where she might be, I wasn't so crazy with worry and dark forebodings as I had been before. Even though we'd been growing apart, each of us immersed in our own mainly drug-related problems, I realised, too, just how much I missed her, and I wanted her back with me badly. But the whole situation was out of my control and there were few options open to me, beyond what I'd tried already. All I could do was to keep on hustling, scoring little bits of skag and methadone here and there, trying to keep the sickness and the nightmares at bay until my luck changed for the better.

• • •

It was another week or so before I finally heard from her. An unstamped letter with my name on it was lying on the hallway mat one morning, and I immediately recognised the hand-writing as Cissy's. I quickly tore open the envelope, hoping to find a lengthy and detailed explanation of where she had been and what she had been doing, together with notice of her immi-nent return; but instead, all I got was a scribbled note with instructions to meet her the following afternoon at a certain West End pub. I briefly wondered who had posted the letter through our door, whether it was Cissy or some unknown friend — but the important thing was that she had contacted me, and all the questions and explanations could wait until the next afternoon.

Thursday was Giro day, and I got up early to cash the cheque, then blew the lot on a half-gramme of smack. I felt good as I took the 29 bus down to Charing Cross Road — I'd actu-ally showered and changed my stinking clothes for the first time in days and was feeling more like a human being than I'd felt in a long time. As I crossed Cambridge Circus and entered the pub, I couldn't see any sign of Cissy, so I bought a drink then sat down to wait. I'd been there for about ten minutes when she walked in through the swing doors, sporting a pair of shades, and with her hair tied back in a ponytail that bobbed from left to right as she scanned the pub looking for me. She was wearing high heels and a silver lurex top that clearly showed the outlines of her nipples, under a black fur coat that I had never seen before; and though she was pale and thin — and looked very strung-out — to me, at that moment, she was the most beautiful woman in the world, and I felt my cock getting hard as I looked at her. She caught sight of me and smiled briefly, then breezed over to where I was sitting as if she were a model on the catwalk, oblivious to the stares and raised eyebrows of the office workers and secretaries on lunchbreak. She leaned over and kissed me on the cheek, like it had been only a couple of hours, instead of over a month, since we'd last seen each other. Then she sat down beside me, removing her sunglasses as she did so and placing them on the table in front of us. Her eyes, I noticed, were very pinned.

"So what's new? I heard you got ripped off by that bastard Dodgy Dave . . . what the fuck were you doin' scoring through him anyway? I ought to be pissed off at you — that was my money, or at least Julia's, that you lost there. Jesus, you look a mess!"

Typically, Cissy had totally wrong-footed me. I'd been expecting her to be on the defensive for doing a disappearing act and taking half of the money and the methadone with her. Instead, she had gone straight onto the attack, fazing me completely.

"I was desperate. There was a serious smack shortage at the time, if you remember . . . No fucker was able to cop anywhere, and Dave was the only one who managed to suss out anything at all. Maybe if I'd had a bit of methadone left, I wouldn't have had to score through him."

"Fuck off! That was my money, remember? I left you half, an' it's not my fault you went an' gave it all to some crook like Dodgy Dave. Look, I don't want to get into this again, recriminations an' blame all the time, that's why I left in the first place — that an' your bloody selfishness. You can be a right bastard at times . . . Anyway, I've missed you, shithead, more than you could ever know — but there's another reason I've had to stay away. Dougie's been released from Peterhead, an' he's back in London, an' he's lookin' for me . . ."

"I know, I ran into him one night when I was passing by your old place. Nice looking bloke, your ex-old man."

"Oh Jesus!" Cissy went even paler, if that was possible. "He didn't follow you, did he? The guy's a fuckin' psycho, an' I know he wants me back. I know how he thinks, an' as far as he's concerned I'm still his old lady, an' if he susses that I'm with you, that's both of us finished."

"I'm not scared of 'im — an' anyway, I lost him around the back of King's Cross. He's not so fast, an' he looks like a fuckin' neanderthal, I bet his brain's even slower than his feet." I didn't really believe this — I hadn't forgotten the penetrating eyes, the feeling of intuitive, predatory intelligence that I had picked up on — but I wanted to impress Cissy and make her feel safe, let her see that she didn't need to worry, that I would always be there to look after her. My words had totally the opposite effect.

"Are you crazy?! You've never seen 'im stomp anyone, but I have, an' it isn't a pretty sight, believe me. The guy fuckin' loves violence, feeds off it, he goes into another world completely, an' I bet he's even worse after a few years in the nick. Promise me you won't square up to him if you run into him again, he's always carryin' a blade an' he's not afraid to use it — just don't wind him up, whatever you do. Jesus, I'm gonna have to go an' see him, sort things out between us — he's been goin' around all our old connections asking after me, an' it's only a matter of time before he twigs who you are, an' where we live. Shit, why'd I ever have to get involved with 'im in the first place?!"

I didn't want Cissy going anywhere near this nutter, and tried to persuade her against it. I wanted her back with me right away, but she was adamant that first she had to smooth things out with Dougie, make him see that their relationship was over, just as she had done with Jed the biker. I wondered, briefly, why I always seemed to be attracted to crazy women who were somehow involved with total psychos — I'd been in similar situations a couple of times in New York — but I let the thought pass. I had other things on my mind.

"So what have you been doin' for money, an' where've you been staying, if I'm allowed to ask?"

For the first time, Cissy did look slightly defensive.

"Oh, champagne hustling in one of the clubs in Soho. You know, tourists and sad old fucks who come here looking for good times, an' get totally ripped off. Basically, you talk to 'em for half an hour, get 'em to order a bottle of champagne, then they get hit with a bill of about a hundred quid, an' you get a commission on it. I did feel a bit guilty about doin' it at first, but it's good money, an' anyway it's their own stupid fault — anyone who steps into one of these dives needs their head examinin'. Ali put me onto it, an' I've been stayin' at her place to avoid Dougie."

"Who's Ali?"

"Oh, I've known her for ages, I met her in Holloway — she used to be on the game, an' her pimp was a dealer too, a real gruesome little fuck. But she's rid of him now, and she's cleaned up her act. She's really helped me out a lot, gettin' me this job an' puttin' me up at her place — it's out of the area, an' Dougie doesn't know anything about her."

A thousand questions raced through my mind, but I knew better than to ask. We'd just end up in a flaming row again, which was the last thing I wanted right now.

"Ali was the one who put the note through the door. I heard you were goin' around like Joe the Gumshoe with some 'orrible old picture of me, asking questions, so I thought I'd better get in touch. An' I have missed you babe, honest. Look, don't look so miserable — everything'll work out fine, just wait an' see. Anyway, I've got a mate with a flat around the corner, an' I've arranged for her to be out for the afternoon, so let's stop yappin' about the ifs, buts an' maybes, and go an' have a good time!"

I took the hint and kept my mouth shut. I hadn't had sex in ages, and the more wasted Cissy got, the more beautiful she looked to me. We spent the rest of the afternoon in bed, and when it was time for her to leave for work at the club, she gave me Ali's phone number and a hundred and fifty pounds in cash. It felt like prostitution in reverse, but I wasn't complaining. The more messed up we both got, the more impossible the situation, the more truly I seemed to love her — an intense and doomed love that burned my heart and went on forever, the only thing left (apart from smack), that could lift my spirit above the dross that existence had now become.

• • •

Days passed, and there was no further news from Cissy. I tried calling her a couple of times at Ali's, but the answer machine was always on, and as there was no phone in our squat she couldn't return my calls. I didn't want to pressure her anyhow — she obviously needed some space to sort out her affairs, and though I was worried about her meeting with Dougie, it was her decision and I had to respect it. And so I carried on in my own happy way, copping for other people while always taking a little extra "commission" for my efforts. It was a miserable existence and I was sick more often than I was high, and finally I began to think about getting onto some kind of methadone maintenance or reduction programme. I'd always avoided doing this in the past, firstly because it meant registering with the Home Office as an addict, and secondly I basically hated the stuff. In the States, it usually comes in "biscuit" form, or is dissolved in orange juice, while in England it is prescribed as a linctus: a thick, sweet-tasting, green liquid that resembles cough mixture and is loaded with sugar. It certainly works, and half an hour after drinking it you feel a warm glow start to spread outwards from your stomach to all the other parts of your body — a high that resembles that of heroin, but without the flash, or the rush, that comes when you shoot smack.

The effects also last longer than gear, and one dose of 30-40 mls. will keep you straight for twenty four hours; but although I had often used it in the past to get through times of heroin shortages, or when I'd had to go away from the city for any length of time and couldn't cop, I had always promised myself that I would never use it on a regular basis. It is actually far harder to kick than heroin, and if you develop a methadone habit it takes weeks rather than days for the withdrawal symptoms to end. Even if you gradually reduce to 5 mls. a day, and then come off — which is what you are supposed to do — the stuff hangs around in your system for so long that thirty six hours later withdrawal will begin; and though it might not be as intense as if you go cold turkey straight from using half a gramme of smack a day, it seems to go on forever: two to three weeks of endless aches, chills, sweats and sleepless, pain-wracked nights.

I once read, or heard somewhere, that it was invented by Nazi scientists during the Second World War, under orders from Göring and other high-ranking officers who were themselves strung-out on morphine. Worried about maintaining shipments of opium from the east, as they began to lose the war and supply lines were cut, they ordered research to be carried out as a matter of urgency. The docs. came up with a synthetic, opiate-like painkiller, which they called "Adolophin," in honour of the Führer, and which could be used as a morphine substitute in military hospitals. And though I'm not one hundred percent sure of the accuracy of this story, and it may be just part of junkie lore, methadone (as it was sensitively renamed), is like some kind of final solution to the problem of bodily and mental pain: a living fucking death that makes you more like a zombie than a human being, the ultimate drug of social control, and one long-favoured by the government and medical establishment as a way of dealing with a rising junkie population while keeping the crime rate down. It takes away your energy, your desire to live, and you will sit quite happily all day long in a darkened room, watching a flickering TV screen without a thought or idea in your head. And methadone, far more than heroin, kills the human sex drive, numbing your body and mind to the point where you don't feel anything at all. True, it "stabilizes" you, and in conjunction with counselling and support can do some good; but if this is the aim, then why not administer exact doses of pharmaceutical heroin and clean syringes to those junkies who either can't stop using, or want to come off and reduce gradually? Obviously, because the media would have a field day with politicians having to answer difficult questions over "Junkies Getting High On The NHS." Methadone, as part of a closely-monitored drug rehabilitation programme, is better than nothing; but as junkies are expert liars, they will always manage to con doctors into giving them larger amounts than they really need, selling the rest on the street to buy more smack. Certainly, that's what I intended to do when I took a bus ride over to Kilburn one day to register with Doctor Mitchell.

Doc. Mitchell was actually a nice guy who believed sincerely in the efficacy of the methadone reduction cure. He wasn't only in it for the money, like a lot of these private quacks, and he was basically a liberal with a social conscience who thought he was doing some good. But I'd heard from other junkies that he was a soft touch, and easy to con, and so I went there fully intending to hit him up for as much methadone as I could possibly get.

During the interview, I exaggerated the extent of my habit so that I would start off on a high dose, and I said all the right things about manic depression, a troubled childhood, emotional problems and difficult relationships that social workers and shrinks love to hear — confirming, as it does, everything they've read in books and studied at medical school or university. I also convinced him of my heartfelt and sincere desire to come off drugs, that I'd had enough of all that, that I'd finally met a "nice" girl who wanted me to get off gear and move in with her. It was a once-in-a-lifetime opportunity that such a girl had come along at a moment in time when I was ready to stop using, and if I didn't seize this chance now I could envisage myself sliding ever deeper into a life of substance abuse and crime, probably leading to severe health problems and an early, ignominious death.

"I don't want to end up like that," I told him with tears in my eyes, almost believing my own story. "She's a wonderful girl, and I really think she can give me the emotional stability I need to kick the habit once and for all. If I don't do it now, then I never will — I really want to stop, but I realise I need help and counselling, and I want to go on a methadone reduction cure so that I can move in with her and distance myself from the drug scene altogether. I don't want to let her down — but even more importantly, I don't want to let myself down."

Doc. Mitchell searched my face closely with his soft brown eyes, and for a moment I did feel a pang of guilt — but only for a moment. This was an open-and-shut case of survival, a way back into dealing that I couldn't afford to waste, and I wasn't about to blow it. Finally, the doc. seemed to make up his mind that I was on the level, telling me to report back in ten days for a second appointment, just to show that I was really serious about wanting to embark on the programme (boy, was I!). He would decide then what dosage of methadone I should start on, after the analysis of my urine sample had come back from the laboratory. (Knowing this was coming, I'd gathered all my resources and had taken a particularly large hit that morning.) We were both pleased with the results of the interview, and as I walked back towards Kilburn High Road I felt strangely purged, and not a little holy, as if in confessing my sins I had somehow liberated myself, even though my whole spiel had been a pack of lies from start to finish.

When I returned ten days later, Doctor Mitchell put me on a script of 60 mls. a day, which I could collect from the Kilburn branch of Bliss's Chemist, one week's supply at a time. This was to be reduced at a rate of 5 mls. after the first fortnight, and thereafter at one-weekly intervals — which didn't bother me too much: I felt sure I'd be able to arrange a little relapse when the supply got too low, and convince the good doctor to reinstate me at a higher dosage once again. And so, half an hour later, I walked out of Bliss's Chemist with over 400 mls. of methadone in my hands, ready to be sold and converted into smack.

• • •

Somehow, she didn't look the same anymore. Outwardly, yes, she was the same beautifully wasted Cissy that I'd last seen in the West End only a few weeks before; but inside, something indefinable had changed, as if some part of her essential spirit had been sucked out, leaving only a hollow facsimile, a fragile and brittle shell.

When I'd arrived home, after returning from some dubious mission, to find her sitting on the bed in our room, for an instant I'd failed to recognise her, so different did she seem; and the weary, listless way in which she'd greeted me made me feel like I was speaking to her ghost, not the real Cissy at all. She looked worn out, and there were big, dark circles under her eyes as if she had not slept for days. Everything about her seemed somehow shrunken — not in a physical sense, but as though something inside her had given up the fight and was now collapsing inwards, silently and invisibly. True, I'd seen her depressed and withdrawn before and, like me, she often had black moods that went on for days at a time — but this was obviously something different. It was as if her energy had changed — not just the level or intensity, but rather the quality itself was different, and I felt intuitively, with a horrible sinking feeling in my stomach, that from now on it was all over: not only for the relationship between us, but for Cissy herself, as a person.

I tried to draw her out and get her to talk to me, tell me about what had happened, but she wasn't interested. All she kept saying was how tired she felt, that we'd talk things over in the morning, and eventually we both fell asleep — not in each other's arms as usual, but on opposite sides of the bed, cold and remote, each of us in our own separate, darkly churning worlds.

The next day it was the same: she didn't want to talk. She just sat around chain-smoking all day, only breaking this routine to take a shot, one in the morning and one at night, from a bag of smack that I reckoned must have weighed at least five or six grammes. The champagne-hustling business must be kicking, I thought to myself sarcastically; but to be fair, she did offer me a hit each time, and I did accept. I certainly wasn't going to turn down the offer of a freebie . . .

Again we went to bed without talking, and each time I tried to make contact Cissy brushed me off, finally turning over and freezing me out completely just as she had done the night before. It was driving me crazy: for weeks I'd been looking forward to having her back with me, but now that she was, she seemed even more remote and unreachable than she had been when she was physically absent. I felt like just grabbing her, taking her against her will if necessary. Sex was actually the least part of it — I felt angry and frustrated at being unable to break through the silence that enclosed her, and the tension between us was unbearable. I wanted to puncture it, to bring things to a head by some gross act of physical or sexual violence; but I realised, at the same time, that something pretty cataclysmic must have happened to make her act in such a way, and that perhaps a little sensitivity on my part was called for. I ended up in an angry sulk on my side of the bed, unable to sleep and with murderous fantasies flashing through my brain, imagining all the things that she wasn't telling me. I knew that patience and understanding were the qualities I most needed right now, but instead I felt like throttling her.

Finally, on the third day, she seemed to come to some kind of decision, shaking herself out of her torpor and coming over to sit next to me on the bed. We'd been dipping more and more deeply into the bag of gear, and we were both pretty loaded — looking back, I guess this was the only way she could handle telling me what was in her mind.

"Look, I guess we should talk about all of this . . ."

"Yeah, I guess we should . . ."

"For fuck's sake, don't go all sarcastic on me, I just can't take that right now — either we're gonna talk straight, or not at all."

I'd wanted truth and honesty, but now I wasn't so sure . . .

"So, let's talk . . ."

"Look, I know it's been tough on you the last few weeks, an' I'm sorry, but believe me, it's been a fuck of a lot harder for me. When I first heard that Dougie was out of nick, I went a bit crazy, I suppose . . . You know the way it ended between us, it was so fucked-up, an' we never saw each other after the bust, except in court — nothing was ever really resolved . . ."

"So now you want to go back to him . . ."

"Shut up and listen, will you! At first, I was shit-scared he would find me, that's why I took off and stayed with Ali — I thought he blamed me for the bust, and was on some kind of revenge trip, especially when I heard he was askin' after me all over the place. Anyway, you know this part of the story, an' you probably think I was doin' all kinds of fucked-up things to get money for gear . . . but really, I was just pushin' champagne to these sad, lonely old bastards . . ."

"Mmmm . . ." I couldn't help myself. I knew the scene too

well, and about how the girls who worked in it could make a little extra money if they wanted to. Cissy shot me a murderous look, but then carried on regardless.

"Anyway, that isn't important — you do what you have to do, you know that as well as I do. An' you also know that I fuckin' love you, so just leave it alone. What is important, is that in spite of the way I feel, I can't be together with you anymore, it's just not gonna work out — I'm sorry, but there it is, I've said it now, an' there's no turning back. Jesus, you're better off without me anyway, you were doin' okay until you ran into me again. Christ, why am I doomed to have this effect on every guy I'm with?! I either turn them into psychos, or destroy them, or both . . ."

She looked as though she wanted to weep, but no tears came to her eyes. Maybe she had cried them all already; or maybe it was just the smack, insulating and deadening her emotions. For myself, in spite of sensing what was coming, and in spite of the gear, I felt like my stomach had dropped into my boots. I looked at her closely, but it was as if she were on automatic pilot now — her eyes were wide and unseeing, staring vacantly at the floor in front of her, and she spoke in a flat, dull monotone, without feeling or inflection.

"So, anyway, after goin' round the twist for a few weeks, thinkin' he was looking for me to do me in, I decided to go an' see him, sort things out one way or the other. I couldn't stand it anymore, I seem to have been runnin' all my fuckin' life . . . plus, I was worried about you as well, believe it or not . . ."

"You've told me this bit already . . ."

". . . So, I finally tracked him down, livin' in this crappy little bedsit in Somerstown. It's like a rabbit cage, small an' dark, hardly room to move, an' we talked an' talked about the bust, an' what went down after — an' it's true what I thought, it was 'cos of me an' my big fuckin' mouth . . ."

"Or he's tryin' to guilt-trip you back to him . . ."

". . . he knows who it was tipped off the Ol' Bill, it was someone I was blabbin' on to, an' I guess he got well paid for his trouble — but anyway, Dougie's not goin' after him or nothin', to him it's water under the bridge now. It's just so sad, that's all, an' it's all my fuckin' fault that he's gonna die . . ."

"Hang on a minute, you've lost me here — who's gonna die?"

"Dougie is — basically, he got HIV from sharin' dirty needles while he was in the nick, an' his T-cell count is up an' down like a yo-yo — it could go into full-blown AIDS at anytime, an' it's all my fuckin' fault, don't you see? God, he used to be so strong, an' now he's like an old man, scared but resigned, not even bitter about it all, it's just so horrible . . . I wish he would get violent, at least I could understand that . . ."

I felt shocked and sad, angry, hopeless and confused, all at the same time. I looked at Cissy sitting there beside me, with her pale skin and her dark eyes drained of all expression, and I wanted her back with me, like it had been before everything got so fucked-up. Maybe it had been fucked-up all along, but I wanted to make her see that it wasn't her fault, that it was just life and the way the dice fell; but I also knew her paranoid way of thinking, and that it would be impossible to ever convince her of this. I'd never met anyone so frightened, so convinced of their own culpability as she was — like she said, she had been running all her life, and I could see that at last she had gone over the emotional edge that I had been trying to pull her back from for so long. I felt the hopelessness of it all, and I felt the evil rising in me, like a poisonous snake in the pit of my stomach; I could feel it coming, maybe I could even have stopped it if I'd wanted to. But I didn't want to: if it had to be over, then it had to be really over — if I couldn't get Cissy back, then I'd give her one final push and jump right after her into the stinking pit myself. The snake came into my mouth, opened its dripping jaws, and spoke:

"So, did Dougie tell you all this before you let him fuck you, or afterwards?"

Cissy looked at me in disbelief for a moment, then her face twisted in contempt. I saw the punch coming, but made no attempt to dodge it, and her tiny fist slammed into my mouth, actually drawing blood. All the uncertainty, pain and frustration of the previous few weeks welled up inside me, and without stopping to think, I punched her right back.

"You fucking bastard! I used to think you were different from all the other psychos I seem to attract, that you had a soul, an' that you really cared about me. Well more fool me — you're even more of a cunt than the rest. At least I could see it coming with them, it was all upfront — whereas you've kept it back until I'm down on my knees, then hit me with every-thing you've got, you rotten scum-bag! Well, in answer to your question, that's for me to know an' for you to find out. Jesus, I wish I had fucked you the last couple of nights, then you'd really have something to think about! Yeah, underneath you're just like all the other twisted, junkie psychos I've had the pleas-ure to know and love, it's just sex an' drugs to you, that's all that matters! Well, you've taken plenty of sex from me, fucked me up well an' truly, so you might as well take the last bit of drugs, as well. Here, take it, it's yours!"

With that, she flung what was left of the bag of heroin onto the floor at my feet, then stood up and walked out of the room. For a few minutes I sat staring into space, in shock, unable to believe what had been said, and what had come to pass. Then I reached down, picked up the packet of gear from the floor and emptied a good-sized shot into the spoon which lay waiting on the table. My hands were shaking, and I badly needed a hit to steady my nerves.

DURING THE LAST FOUR MONTHS, since my big bust-up with Cissy, the situation in the house has been sliding increasingly out of control. For the first few days after she left, I stayed as high as possible, not wanting to face up to the fact that our relationship was over, and grateful for the emotional numbness that the methadone and smack bestowed upon me. Even so, I could feel the emptiness, the pain of loss throbbing away beneath the drugs, and I dreaded the time when I would have to deal with it unaided and alone.

I'd figured that I wouldn't see her again, other than when she came to collect her possessions, but about a week after the row she walked in, just as I was about to get high with about half a dozen other people. Gradually, through hustling and selling most of my methadone, I'd started to deal smack again, although on a much-reduced scale; and once more, our room was home to a constant procession of assorted characters waiting to cop, or trying to get rid of stolen goods of one kind or another.

Her manner was brusque and businesslike, and she completely ignored the others, addressing only me when she spoke.

"I've come to get my things. I'm moving in downstairs, into Pete's old room, so I'll need my bed an' the dressing table. I'd appreciate it if you could help me carry 'em downstairs, please."

"What, right now? Do you mind if I take my shot first?" I wasn't only being sarcastic. Cissy's unexpected appearance, and her announcement that she intended to move back into the squat, had totally floored me; I was also annoyed that she had walked in on a roomful of my friends and was putting a dampener on everybody's high with her proud and arrogant attitude. To be fair, she probably felt awkward too and was maybe just over-compensating. I took my shot and felt a little better, but it was hard and unnatural to be nonchalant as we manoeuvered Cissy's queen-sized bed down the narrow, twisting stairway. Too many feelings were welling up inside me, and I didn't trust myself to speak. We moved the heavier articles of furniture in silence, then Cissy came back up and carried the lighter things, her jewellery, clothes and records, by herself.

I returned to my room, where Steve, Eddy and the others sat waiting, and we continued to get high for the rest of the afternoon. We all thought it was a strange move on Cissy's part, wanting to come back to the squat, and we discussed it briefly — what it could mean, and what it would lead to — while a few jokes were made at my expense about needing a new bed. But then we forgot about it (or at least they did), and we carried on drinking the bottle of Scotch that someone had brought along, getting high until the early hours of the morning.

I bumped into Cissy a few times over the following days, on the staircase or coming in the front door from the street, but neither of us spoke, and it was as if we had never known each other at all. It was an absurd situation, but there was no getting around it — too much had happened and too many things had been said to go back now, even if we had wanted to.

I learned from some friends that Cissy had fallen out with Ali and had nowhere to stay — that was why she had moved back into the squat — and not only that: Julia had somehow discovered that the money she'd loaned to her had all been blown on gear, and had thrown a fit. No doubt, in her mind, Cissy blamed me for this latter misfortune, for destroying her wonderful friendship with Julia, and this further compounded the growing feeling of enmity between us. Even though I would have liked to re-establish contact, there seemed to be no way — the same pride, or stubbornness, in each of us prevented any softening of heart, and we both put up a wall of silence whenever we met by chance or necessity.

I soon found out the way things were going to go, and the way they have been going ever since. More and more crazed-looking people began to arrive at the house, and it didn't take me long to realise that Cissy had gone into direct competition with me, selling smack, cocaine and speed from her room downstairs. That actually didn't bother me so much — she had her customers and I had mine, and anyhow there was no way I could realistically compete with her: she had a large amount of capital at her disposal that she had made one way or another, while I was still surviving on a day-to-day, shot-by-shot basis.

It was the amount of traffic coming to the house that worried me. I had always tried to limit the number of people passing through by keeping strict hours, refusing to deal at night unless it was a special favour to a friend who was sick. Now, there were people arriving and leaving twenty four hours a day, while there was always some kind of party going on in one of the rooms — drugs, sex, or both — full of strange, unknown characters, any one of whom could have been a stoolie or police informer. I was getting more and more paranoid, convinced that we were about to be busted. The cops would have a field day: they could lock us all up on any number of counts, from the use and sale of illegal substances, through being knowledgeable receivers of stolen goods, to less serious offences such as underage sex and freely tapping into the municipal gas and electricity supplies. It was a sledgehammer-through-the-door, sniffer-dogs-and-handcuffs situation waiting to happen, and I wasn't happy about it at all.

The trouble was, I was as much to blame as anyone. The pale, sleazy, vampirical creatures who visited me were hardly less noticeable, in their own way, than the variously deranged and intense-looking characters who visited other parts of the house, often staying for days at a time. As Cissy appeared determined to run some kind of non-stop, twenty-four-hours-a-day drugs supermarket, I decided to go along with the general flow of things, and completely gave up trying to preserve any kind of anonymity. I basically accepted that we were going to be busted in the not too distant future, and in my darker moods

I would almost welcome the prospect as a way out of the blind alley that my life had become. But amazingly, it never happened; and even though it must have been obvious to anyone who was half awake that this was no ordinary squat, and that strange things were happening within, the anticipated police raid never arrived.

The most interesting transformation, though, has been in Cissy herself. I always knew that she had a streak of selfishness and greed in her; but in the past this was always balanced by her warmth and energy, her infectious sense of enthusiasm that could sweep people along, making life with her unpredictable and interesting, if nothing else. Now, this lighter side has disappeared completely. Something cold and grasping has begun to emerge, something in her that is almost insect-like in the way she stays in her room all day, dealing from her bed and holding court to her customers like a skagged-out version of decrepit old Miss Havisham from *Great Expectations*. She hoards and protects her gear like some dark, underworld creature with its eggs, doling it out in obsessively weighed and measured amounts to her customers, who seem to be more like disciples, or drones around a queen bee, rather than normal run-of-the-mill junkie types. Many dealers get on power trips, it's true, and take an active enjoyment in making people wait, or watching them crawl; but Cissy has elevated this tendency to an art form. Sometimes I walk past her half-open door and I catch her image reflected in the large, oval mirror on top of the dressing table, sat up in bed with her scales, packets of gear, spoons and syringes scattered about, surrounded by six or seven pale-faced young guys. Junkie castratos in the court of Queen Cissy, they hang on her every word and are only too willing to run errands for her, to flatter her in every way possible. A couple of months back, she had long, blond hair-extensions fitted that hang in braids almost to her arse, the type that are all the rage in the London clubs right now. With her pale skin and false hair, dressed in a white shift and propped up on pillows, she really does look like some twisted version of a Victorian child's doll, translucent and ageless, but with an undertone of disease and malice behind the ivory smoothness of her flawless, junkie skin.

I don't know why, but some people, especially young girls, seem to thrive for a time on heroin. It wastes them, sure, but it also increases their beauty in some alien or waif-like way, and Cissy is undoubtedly of this type, her pretty looks now having reached some kind of apotheosis of weird, strung-out beauty. Of course, what is given is also taken back later, and with interest. Heroin seems to act almost like a preservative, holding back time and allowing the user to remain young and ageless, as if in suspended animation, and a junkie who is thirty five, or even forty years old, can easily be mistaken for someone in their early twenties. The problem actually comes when you stop taking the drug. In the same way that years of blocked emotions suddenly bubble to the surface in a mixed up mess of pain, remorse and confusion, so the aging process will attack your body with a vengeance, as your metabolism struggles to readjust and years of chemically-induced imbalance must be paid for. In the first year after kicking, many ex-users become fat and bloated, while on an almost daily basis you will notice new lines appearing on your face, a map wherein can be read all your previous sins and transgressions; and although this doesn't always happen, the appearance of some ex-junkies does bring to mind the picture of Dorian Gray in the attic, or the face of some Hollywood vampire who has been unexpectedly delayed and caught by the rays of the rising sun.

The trouble is, that as much as I loathe this new insect-like Cissy and her fucked-up, bitchy ways, I still want her. I've been seeing other girls lately, but the feeling I get with them just isn't the same as what I had with Cissy, and as much as I fight it, the truth is that I'm still obsessed with her.

First, there was the French girl who moved into the basement, a damp and stinking wreck of a room that she cleaned up with the help of some anonymous old man. In the beginning, I thought he was her father; later that he was a trick who she fucked for money. At any rate, I haven't seen him for a long time now, not since he finished redecorating her room. One night a few months back she came upstairs to buy some speed off me and we ended up spending the night together. It was okay, as casual sex goes, but I soon found out that she was into leather and S&M, and what really turned her on was to be fucked in the arse while she masturbated her clitoris, or rubbed it against some piece of furniture, a wooden chair-arm or the rounded end of a bedpost. Of course, this was interesting, and I went along with it all quite happily, but the trouble was she couldn't have an orgasm any other way — when I fucked her in the cunt, she wanted me to come as quickly as possible (pretty difficult when you're loaded on gear), saying that my cock made her sore and that she had never been able to orgasm this way. Yet she was quite content to have me fuck her hard up the arse for as long as I wanted, while she masturbated and watched our reflection in the mirror. She especially enjoyed wearing a tight leather corset with a dog collar and chain around her neck, and as she began to climax she liked me to pull hard on this while I fucked her from behind, so that at the peak of her orgasm she felt that she was being strangled to death. She also liked to be hit hard on the bare arse with a wooden paddle or a leather belt, or gagged with a ball and chain device while I slapped her face and called her all the sexually derogatory names I could think of — something that made me want to laugh, but which really seemed to turn her on. I must admit that I enjoyed these scenes too, and participated enthusiastically — people are strange, and I long ago gave up on the idea that there is any such thing as "normal" sex. But to be truthful, she irritated the hell out of me when we weren't in bed together, and without any love or deeper feeling on either side this lustful but limited affair soon burned itself out and became an empty ritual, repetitious and ultimately boring.

There were a couple of other one night stands, but for the last two months now I've been seeing Vikki, a beautiful young English-Chinese girl from Bristol who has aspirations to be a photographer and film-maker. She's a lovely fuck, and for some unknown reason appears to be crazy about me; and, compared to most of the girls I attract, she seems incredibly well-organised and together, cooking meals for me when I forget to eat, and making sure I don't use someone else's dirty old syringe that has been left lying around. She's very conscious of the risk of HIV and even makes me wear a condom when we fuck — which is, I suppose, a sensible move on her part, me being in a particularly high-risk group, after all.

I love the way she sucks on my lower lip, and bucks and grinds into me when she comes, soaking the bed with her juices. Her long, black hair cascades down over her shoulders, the ends of it teasing each pink and upturned nipple, while her body and face glisten with a silver sheen of sweat as I lick and fuck her to orgasm. If I'm above her when she comes, I love to watch her thick, red lips pull back from her teeth, like some primitive and pornographic mask of sexual torture; if I'm between her legs, then afterwards my hair and face will be soaked, as if someone had thrown a bucket of steaming water over me, but fulsome and rich with her animal scent.

I can tell that she cares about me, and I know that she's good for me, but the trouble is I can't stop thinking about Cissy — and I guess Vikki knows this, because they absolutely loathe each other (Vikki calls her "Spider-Woman"). Now, she seems to have got it into her head that I only ever loved Cissy because she was so fucked-up, that it was her "wildness" and "decadence" that interested me, and a few weeks ago she asked me if I would shoot her up with smack, just so she could "see what it feels like". Of course I refused; but then she got hold of a set of works from somewhere and tried to inject herself with the speed I'd given her, thinking that she only wanted to sniff a line. She made a real mess of her arm, and when I tried to stop her she went kind of crazy, yelling at me to leave her alone, then running downstairs and locking herself in the bathroom. There, she continued to find a vein, while I hammered on the door and tried to reason with her, all to no avail. Eventually I gave up and kicked it in. I found her sitting on the toilet, tears streaming down her face and blood down her virgin arms, still wildly stabbing at herself in manic frustration at not being able to find a vein. She only stopped when I promised that if she came back upstairs with me, I would give her a little gear and inject it for her properly.

Cissy came out of her room to see what all the noise was about, and when she saw the state that Vikki's arms were in, she made some bitchy comment about "stupid little girls" trying to be cool. Vikki flew at her in a rage, with her long, red fingernails aimed directly at Cissy's throat, and I had to pull her back, even though I felt like punching Cissy myself. But in a way, Cissy was right; and after I'd reluctantly given Vikki what she wanted, I could feel only pity and contempt for her pathetic, childish display (and anger at myself for being blackmailed into giving someone their first ever shot, something which I had always promised myself I would never do). Since then, I just can't take her seriously, even though she tries so hard. Maybe she's just too young, but the things she says sound stupid and false to me now — all this bullshit about "experience" and "exploring life" — and I see that behind the facade she's just as fucked-up and neurotic as everybody else.

As for Cissy, she seems to get more crazed, evil and twisted by the day. For awhile, she had a new boyfriend, the sound engineer of a well-known Australian rock band, and I would hear them fucking sometimes, or arguing, as I passed their room on my way to the bathroom, or down the hallway to the front door. Soon, the sounds of love grew less, their arguments got louder and more frequent, and it was obvious that they were having problems as Cissy's tyranny of smack began to take over. From all the shouting I heard, it seemed that JC was being verbally scourged and lashed into some kind of emotional and mental submission. His ever increasing need for gear, plus the fact that Cissy was becoming more and more avid in protecting her stash, meant that they were on a direct collision course; and it wasn't long before he began stealing from her, sneaking up the darkened stairway in the middle of the night to use my facilities in exchange for a share of the stolen goods. In spite of the fact that he was with the woman who, in some way, I was still obsessed with, we became good friends and would sit up together all night long swapping junkie tales and lore, while Cissy slept on downstairs, blissfully unaware that her latest stash place had been rumbled. Of course, in the morning, when she discovered that her golden-brown hoard had been mysteriously depleted overnight by anything up to half a gramme, there would be a furious row, with accusations and recriminations flying in all directions. But JC, being a crafty old fox, always kept a little emergency stash for these occasions when, out of anger or spite, Cissy would cut off his supply — just enough to keep himself straight until he could worm his way back into her good books once again. She began to hide her gear in small amounts in several different places around her room, but somehow JC would always find them; and, biding his time until she went out somewhere, he'd take a little from each, so that in fact this strategy worked against her: it was much harder to detect that these small amounts were missing than it was if a whole lot disappeared at once.

In spite of this underhand and devious behaviour, JC was totally hung-up on Cissy. Both of us were somehow caught in this spider's web — the dark, poisonous side of female sexuality that she was now emanating. And I'm not ashamed to say that we regaled each other mercilessly with tales of her insanity and all-round fucked-up behaviour, as some kind of protection against, or compensation for, the emotional pain that she was capable of inflicting. I began to see her more and more as some kind of insect creature around whom male drones swarmed to suck the nourishing elixir of smack that was secreted; while she, dealing always from her bed, became increasingly obsessive and exact about the quantities of gear she weighed out on her little set of brass scales, taking out then replacing minute amounts until she was fully satisfied that she hadn't given away too much. It was like some primitive form of matriarchy, based on smack, and the worst times were when I couldn't cop anywhere and had to go downstairs to join the queue of ghouls waiting to buy off Cissy. The deals she sold me at such times were always a little under, so I never felt bad about sharing the gear that JC had stolen from her, and we'd sit up until dawn, shooting speed and smack, babbling away until it was time for him to sneak back downstairs and crash out next to Cissy. Hours later, she'd wake to find that yet more of her treasure had unaccountably disappeared.

JC was a one-off, a totally unique character. He was gifted with the driest, blackest sense of humour I have ever come across, and his stories about the criminals and junkie low-life of Melbourne had me in stitches, even though I was in one of the darkest, most miserable periods of my life so far. He was also the most original and talented sound engineer I've ever heard, capable of creating huge, black, cavernous holes of sound for the band he worked with, both in the studio and when they played live. As great as any band might be, live especially, they will only be as good as their soundman; and if he has cloth ears, or doesn't understand the dynamics of their music, no matter how well they might be playing onstage they'll sound like a muddy mess of turgid noise out front to the audience.

Because the audience only hears what is coming through the PA speakers, and this is totally under the control of the sound engineer, stationed at his mixing desk somewhere in the back of the hall, or upstairs in the balcony. A good soundman can pick out the individual instruments to heighten or lower their prominence in the mix, adding colours to the sound and structuring it so that it meshes and holds together; and while it is true that no soundman in the world can make an awful band sound good, it is also true that a bad soundman can make a wonderful band sound like absolute shit. JC was one of the best, and unlike many sound engineers who find the basic levels for each instrument and leave them set like that for the entire performance, he was constantly on the move: adding a little echo here; reverb there; changing the EQ or the volume level of a particular instrument; and generally playing the mixing desk as if he were an additional, but invisible, member of the band — which, in truth, he was.

Unfortunately, he had fallen on hard times, and when he met Cissy he had just been temporarily fired by the band for being the most fucked-up, junked-out and wasted member of a group that was notorious for being fucked-up, junked-out and wasted. It was true that he had become prone to falling asleep at the mixing desk, and was either so stoned, or else so sick, that he eventually became incapable of doing his job properly; so it was no real surprise (except, perhaps, for JC), when he and the band parted ways. Now he was marooned, penniless and thousands of miles from home, with an enormous habit to feed each day and totally at the mercy of Cissy — who had, by this time, turned into a complete virago. With his deep sense of irony and his gallows humour, I suspect it was a situation that JC secretly relished, in a dark, self-mocking kind of way. But it was also obvious that he had reached a dead end as far as his time in London was concerned, and one day he jumped ship with about half of Cissy's stash in his pocket and a one-way ticket back to Melbourne, given to him by the band's record label on condition that he never return. She could not believe that this had happened, so sure was she that JC was completely under her control: her fury and, to be fair, her grief at his unexpected departure (not to mention that of half of her supply), were awesome to behold.

The situation in the house has worsened ever since. Sometimes, I feel it's like a time bomb waiting to explode its rotting and putrescent contents all over the surrounding neighbourhood, so dark and claustrophobic do its rooms and stairways seem to me now. I miss JC and his crazy stories; the enmity between Cissy and myself has settled into a cold and stony silence; and I've never felt so totally alone and isolated in my whole fucking life, not even during the worst days at the end of my time in New York.

Just lately, I've been thinking a lot about this anyway: about how I started taking drugs in the first place, and why I went down this particular road and, most of all, about where it has led me to now. I refuse to regret any of it. I've had a lot of fun and I've learned a lot of things, but to be honest, I think I've taken it about as far as I possibly can without actually killing myself. (I have, in any case, OD'd several times, turning blue on more than one occasion.) As far as I can see, there are three basic choices open to me right now: kill myself straight off, quick and clean; quit while I'm still ahead; or resign myself to this living fucking death that my life has now become, probably leading to actual physical death in the near or not too distant future.

If I look at Cissy, and then at myself, it is not a pretty sight. We have both become, in our own ways, something a little less than "human": she, a bitter, disappointed and twisted bitch, somehow old before her time; me, an emotionally stunted and cold-hearted bastard, perverse and self-defeating. A horrid morass of hatred and self-loathing seems to poison everything within and around us; while both of us are full of these aborted and unrealised possibilities that fester away and rot inside. And Vikki, too . . . I know that my continuing obsession with Cissy is destroying her also, and all that nonsense about shooting herself up was just her way of trying to compete on some hopeless and absurd level. I'm not even that interested in fucking her anymore, even though she has one of the most perfect and sexually-enticing little bodies that I've ever seen, and this is making her even more crazy. (Maybe it's the smack, or more likely the methadone, finally getting to me after all these years.) I just haven't been able to take her seriously ever since that episode in the bathroom, while Cissy's words about "silly little girls trying to be cool" keep on ringing in my ears, like some kind of hex, or hoodoo. It's not really Vikki's fault, I know: she's in way over her head, and can't understand or deal with the situation at all. I just wish she was a little bit older, or had something in her — some mental or emotional power — that could blast and banish this evil witch from my life forever. But it's something I've got to do for myself, I realise that — the only question being, of course: how? I've got two addictions to kick, Cissy and smack, and I'm so far down I can't even see daylight anymore. So where do I get the inner strength and resolution to haul myself back up again, to switch from negative to positive, when all my circuits and wiring are burned out, seemingly beyond repair? ("An interesting and apposite question, Watson, and one that requires not a little thought and cogitation . . .")

Dougie and his psycho brother Tony have been coming around lately — Dougie to visit Cissy, Tony to buy speed off me. Dougie and Tony actually hate each other's guts; but they have the type of fraternal relationship whereby if either one of them is threatened by an outside party, both of them will unite to beat the living shit out of this third, unfortunate and uncautious person. Tony is an out-and-out thug, dangerous and potentially lethal, but Dougie has apparently mellowed; maybe with age and experience; maybe with the knowledge that, carrying the HIV virus as he does, his days are probably numbered. In any case, though you can see that he still has it in him to be a hard and brutal bastard, he also has a soft and almost sensitive side. It's obvious that he still feels protective about Cissy, and that she was mistaken and being totally paranoid when she thought he was looking for her to carry out some form of violent revenge.

He wasn't there to protect her, though, a few weeks ago, when some shady deal she had got herself involved in went horribly wrong. It was a typical kind of Cissy business venture, full of misunderstandings, bad judgement, betrayals, dubious characters, panic and sheer, unadulterated greed. Ever since JC had left with half of her gear, she had been looking for an opportunity to make up the deficit. So when some obscurely connected acquaintances of people she vaguely knew came up from the West Country — with over two thousand pounds in cash — looking to buy speed and an ounce of high-quality heroin, they were put into contact with Cissy, who jumped at the chance to make something out of the deal. The deal was, if she scored the ounce she could use the remaining money to buy herself two or three grammes — worth up to four hundred pounds when cut was added and the smack divided into quarter-gramme packets, each selling for twenty five pounds a throw. Of course, she also intended to cream off a couple of grammes from the full ounce and add a little cut to make up the difference (not so much that anyone would notice . . .); so that altogether she stood to make about six hundred pounds on the venture, just for picking up the gear and handing it over to the buyers — a task that she promised would be accomplished within three or four days at the most.

The problem was that although these people weren't big-time dealers, they were fairly heavy characters, and you could tell by their appearance that they were not the type who would take kindly to being fucked around. I didn't know what was happening, or what Cissy was planning to do, until afterwards; I just saw these three tough-looking guys, not her usual type of customer at all, coming out of her room one day as I passed them on my way up the stairs.

Anyway, it seems that Cissy wasn't able to cop a full ounce anywhere, only a half at maximum. But instead of doing the sensible thing and being straight with the buyers — giving them the choice of having their money back and going elsewhere, or waiting for her until one of her dealers came up with the goods — she decided to go ahead and buy the half, with the intention of making up the full amount later when she could find somewhere else to cop. The disadvantage was, of course, that buying it this way, in two separate deals, she would have to pay a higher price, and so her profit margin would be that much smaller. Consequently, she would have to cut the gear that much more if she still wanted to make the same amount of money out of the deal as she'd originally intended.

Another problem was that having a half ounce of such high-quality smack lying around for a few days was just too much of a temptation. She began to dip into it herself, reasoning that it was such good gear she could easily add quite a large cut later — after she'd scored the other half, that is — and nobody would be any the wiser. It would still be better stuff than anything these "hicks from the sticks" had ever laid their hands on before, of that she was convinced. Somehow, though, word filtered back to these guys that Cissy had copped, and they sent a message that they would be up from the country the next evening to collect; and with this news, Cissy went into panic mode, sending out scouts and hunters to search for another half ounce, then foolishly entrusting one of them with the money when he successfully located a dealer with the requisite amount to sell.

Whether this guy was genuinely ripped off, or did the dirty

on Cissy himself, is open to conjecture: she and her friends were all so loaded on this first batch of particularly good smack that none of them really knew what they were doing during the whole of this time. But the upshot was that he returned with half an ounce of what was basically cut mixed with a little heroin: the kind of stuff which, if you tried to smoke it off silver foil, would crackle and burn black like sugar or baking soda — which, in reality, was what it mostly consisted of.

Cissy's panic increased even more when she weighed out the good stuff and found out that there was just over ten grammes of it remaining. She had been so stoned that she simply hadn't noticed how much was being used — either that, or else one of her friends had been helping himself while she wasn't looking. Her first impulse was to mix the high-quality gear with the crap to produce three quarters of an ounce of passable stuff, and to reimburse the buyers for the missing quarter out of her own capital, admitting that she had been unable to score the full amount. She might just have got away with this strategy if she hadn't been so greedy; but the thought of having to pay back the buyers out of her own money, while having nothing to show for all her efforts, was just too much for her to bear. So she decided upon a second plan of action: she would cut the high-grade stuff 50/50 to produce twenty grammes of reasonably good-quality street gear, then sell it off in weighed quarter-gramme deals to pay back the buyers — or at least show them that she still had their cash and hadn't yet managed to score. At the worst, she would have got herself out of a sticky situation, and if she could convince them that she was only waiting until some prime gear became available, she might still be able to make money on the venture.

The only problem was time: she had less than twenty four hours to sell about eighty quarter-gramme wraps of street gear, a virtual impossibility, even though she put the word out that she was holding excellent stuff, and more than the usual amount of customers did, in fact, show up to score. She tried to stall for more time; but by now the buyers were highly suspicious, and when they arrived the following evening Cissy had only managed to offload about seven or eight grammes. So what they found was half an ounce of unsellable crap; about eight grammes of street-standard gear that couldn't realistically be cut anymore (a few grammes had somehow gone missing in the general panic); and something like seven or eight hundred pounds in cash from the stuff that Cissy had managed to push. Even after they had taken the money and sold the remaining gear, they would still be short of their initial investment, and as they had hoped to make at least two and a half thousand pounds profit on the deal, they were understandably pissed off. These were working-class guys, garage mechanics or something similar, and had probably been saving for months to get the necessary capital together to start dealing in their home town. Now they were furious at being fucked around and, as they saw it, taken for fools and totally ripped off by some skagged-out little junkie girl.

It could have been much worse, but they limited their revenge to taking whatever cash and valuables they could lay their hands on, and to roughing up Cissy and a couple of her customers who happened to be present at the time. They sat them on chairs, tied their hands behind their backs and held knives to their throats, then went through their pockets and through Cissy's bedside table, for cash, gear and jewellery, before slapping them around a bit more and giving Cissy two black eyes. As a parting gesture, one of them took his knife and made as if to slice her face, but instead cut off her prized hair-extensions, throwing them in a pile at her feet. Then all three of them totally trashed her room. Cissy and her friends eventually managed to free themselves, but for her it was all over. Everything, including her self-respect, had gone, and all she had left to look forward to was a long, painful period of

withdrawal and to hustling around like a street junkie for the odd bit of gear that she could manage to buy or scrounge.

• • •

Since then, she seems to have pretty much given up — she doesn't go out anymore, hardly anyone comes to visit, and she just stays in her room the whole day long with the curtains drawn. She doesn't even have the dog to keep her company anymore: Dougie came and took it away because Cissy can hardly look after herself, let alone the dog, which was skin and bone and hadn't been washed or taken for a good walk in months. It seems kind of sad, I know, and I sometimes wonder if the fun-loving, energetic spirit that Cissy used to have is still there, trapped inside the hard insect shell, and whether it will emerge again one day if she ever gets herself off smack and away from the scene. But I have my own problems to worry about, and Cissy and I are just so far apart now that there's no way I could help her anyway.

Last week, someone OD'd badly in my room, very nearly snuffed it in fact, and it really made me stop and think. Of course, I've seen people overdose before and I've been there several times myself, but this was a particularly bad one, plus I also happened to know the guy personally. I mean, it's bad enough watching someone stiff out if you don't know them: it's horrible to watch life slip away, even from a stranger that you don't know or particularly care about. But in this case it was a friend — and not only that, I'd sold him the gear, so there was a certain amount of personal responsibility involved. It's true that everyone in this scene takes their own chances every time they shoot up; and, if you sell heroin, then of course there's always the possibility that someone is going to die from it. But to have it happen right under your nose, and to someone you know and care for, does bring it home to you with a certain amount of force. Maybe the difference is comparable, in some ways, to dropping incendiary bombs on a town full of people you can't see, as opposed to having to strangle each one of them to death with your own bare hands.

Anyway, Roy was an older guy of around thirty eight or forty who had been clean for years and had recently, for some unknown reason, begun to use again. He ran a construction company under the railway arches near Camden Road train station and was normally a customer of Cissy's, though we both knew him well. He used to help us out with materials and tools whenever repairs needed doing on the squat, and when we first moved in there, he and a couple of his employees came over to remove the antique cast-iron fireplaces that were in the downstairs rooms. He gave us a good price for them — they were much in demand by the middle-class homeowners he used to do work for up in Hampstead and Highgate, and he was only too willing to take them off our hands.

On this particular occasion he had come to me to score, Cissy being out of business and steadfastly refusing to open her door to anyone; and when he asked if he could use my room to get off in, I agreed, figuring that he was an old hand at the game and knew what he was doing. The stuff I was holding was good, but not exceptionally so; yet the moment Roy took the needle out of his arm, his eyeballs rolled back inside his skull and he buckled at the knees, collapsing onto the floor like a hundredweight sack of coal. It wasn't a particularly large shot he had taken either, but smack sometimes gets you like that, especially if you only use it occasionally: maybe the stuff is just a little stronger than your body is used to; or perhaps your metabolism is running more slowly than normal, leaving you feeling depressed and not quite up to par that day. But whatever the reason, it was obvious that Roy was out for the count; and not only that — as I ran over to where his crumpled body lay and knelt beside him, I could hear a horrible gurgling noise coming from his throat, while his lips were beginning to turn a definite shade of pale, pale blue.

A couple of other friends, Sid and Jenny, were in the room with me, and we tried everything we could to bring Roy around, but without success. If I'd been a good Boy Scout, alert and well-prepared, I'd have had a few shots of Naltrexone or some other opiate antagonist ready for such emergencies. But I wasn't. I was just a fucked-up small-time junkie loser trying to survive from day to day, and all three of us were freaking now at the prospect of Roy's imminent death. First we tried ice-cubes down the front of his pants (shock therapy if you like), then lifted him up by his arms, trying to make him walk around to keep his blood circulation going. But he was a big guy, and dead weight, and even though there were three of us we could hardly move him, let alone get him to walk. He crumpled again and lay slumped against an armchair, while I slapped his face hard and shouted at the fucker not to die; but by now he was really turning blue, and a long line of drool was dripping from one corner of his mouth. As far as I could see he wasn't breathing at all.

Jenny was crying, and I was feeling pretty close to total panic myself; Sid, though, who knew something about first aid, pulled Roy's legs out from beneath him, so that he was now lying on his back full-length on the floor, then put an ear to his chest, listening for any heartbeat.

"He's still alive, but only just . . . Quick, get a salt shot together and stick it into his mainline, it might just do the trick — I'll give him mouth-to-mouth to get his breathing going again."

I couldn't believe that Sid was being so calm and collected about the whole affair. I was totally losing it at this point, while Jenny was in hysterics, begging Roy not to die; but I did as I was told and prepared the shot, sticking it into the big vein in his left arm, while Sid continued to give him mouth-to-mouth resuscitation and CPR. Suddenly, Roy's eyelids flickered and he coughed, or rather spluttered, and Jenny cried out in joy as he twitched a little then moved his head to one side. But sadly the celebration was premature, a bit like watching Frankenstein's first unsuccessful experiment, and a moment later Roy's breathing faltered once again, leaving him lying corpse-like on the floor.

"Oh Jesus, he's not gonna make it, is he?" I said, more to myself than to anyone else. Sid was still trying artificial respiration, and every once in a while he got me to help him lift Roy into a sitting position so that he could hit him hard on the back, clearing the phlegm and vomit from his mouth to prevent it from going into his lungs and choking him.

By now Roy had been out for at least fifteen minutes, apart from the short time when he had seemed to come around, and I'd more or less given up hope. I began to collect all my gear and paraphernalia together, ready to ditch it over the back wall before the ambulance and cops arrived. Jenny was weeping quietly to herself in one corner of the room; but Sid, trooper that he was, refused to accept defeat and was still crouched down low over Roy, forcing air into his lungs. In between each breath, while he pressed down on Roy's chest to expel the air and maintain circulation, he was muttering to himself, as if it were a prayer or mantra, "Come on you fucker, breathe! Come on you fucker, breathe!" But I had totally given up hope by now and was in shock, not even panicking anymore as I walked to and fro collecting bits and pieces from the table and the floor. The whole situation seemed unreal: Jenny crying in one corner; me walking around tidying up the room; and Sid still working away, muttering to himself over the piece of dead meat in the other corner next to the door. It was as if time had slowed right down and we were all moving in a dream, or underwater, and lethargically I drifted back to where Sid was kneeling to help him lift Roy into a sitting position for one last, half-hearted try.

As we thumped him hard on the back, all at once a yellow spray of vomit came chundering out of his mouth, and almost simultaneously he began to cough, splutter and breathe again, this time on his own. His eyes opened briefly, and though it was obvious that he hadn't a clue where he was, or what had happened, at least he was alive. Even if the cunt had irreversible brain damage, we could at least get him out of the house and back to his own place, and in the morning no-one would be any the wiser about what had happened — least of all Roy who, I figured, would probably be a total vegetable from now on, due to prolonged oxygen starvation of the brain while he was out cold, dying on the carpet.

Miraculously, though, he gradually came to his senses. But he was still nodding out, and we had to keep slapping his face and making him walk around the room to prevent him from slipping back into a coma. Thanks to Sid's refusal to admit defeat, oxygen had continued to reach Roy's brain, and as he began to recover he seemed more embarrassed about his little "faux pas" than anything else and wanted to leave the house quickly, so badly did he feel about nearly stiffing out in front of us. A lot of old junkies have this strange kind of pride about knowing what their limits are, a little like the heavy beer-drinker who will pace himself all night until he has drunk his friends under the table, and I guess Roy felt a little bad about overdosing in the presence of us younger "pups". But I wouldn't let him leave until I was sure that he wasn't going to nod out again once he got home and into his bed — it really would have been a tragedy if he'd died in his sleep after all Sid's hard work getting him back to the land of the living. When he did eventually leave I went with him, and we walked together around the midnight streets so that he could get some fresh air into his lungs, allowing the smack to work its way out of his system.

I've only seen him once since that night, and though it's true he did seem a little more spaced-out and distant than I remember him being before, it could be that he just feels embarrassed about the whole affair and doesn't want to talk or think about it, or even acknowledge that it ever happened. I don't think he realises just how close he came to snuffing it, or how much he owes to Sid — but that's a junkie for you: proud, arrogant, selfish and fucking ungrateful.

• • •

This morning, I got a real shock when I went downstairs to use the bathroom. All through the night Cissy had been having some kind of wild party in her room, the first time in weeks that I'd heard any signs of life coming from inside there at all, and I'd passed a couple of her guests on the stairway as I was going out and they were coming in. The girl, Carol, I vaguely knew as some friend or acquaintance of Cissy's from King's Cross, a dire and fucked-up street prostitute who wouldn't hesitate to rip you off, or stick a knife in your back, if she believed there was anything in the deal for her. I thought of her as a repository for every germ and infestation that the human body was capable of carrying, a walking virus in fact, and that she was hanging out partying with Cissy right now could mean only one thing: she had come across a large sum of money, probably stolen from some trick, had used it to buy gear, and now needed somewhere quick and convenient where she could shoot up and where no questions would be asked. The guy she was with was a tall, muscular, black man who I knew to be her pimp.

Some more people arrived later, but I didn't see who they were — I just heard a lot of laughter and shouting, and I jealously imagined all the heroin and cocaine that was being consumed while I was again down to my last fifty mls. of methadone. When I went to bed at around three a.m. the party was still in full swing, and occasionally I'd hear loud music or gales of rabid laughter whenever someone opened the door of Cissy's room to go to the toilet next door. It was as if she'd been resurrected from the dead after weeks of cold abstinence in her bolted and shuttered burrow, and I imagined her regal now, sitting up in her bed directing the proceedings, dressed all in white and with her rudely severed hair starting to grow back, at last, in tufts and spikes that stuck out at crazy angles from her head. Above all the noise and mayhem, I'd occasionally hear her raucous cackle, or her voice declaiming excitedly, "Listen, listen to me, will you?!" as she attempted to elucidate a point, or tell some amusing story to her assembled company of cohorts.

At around ten a.m. I awoke with the sickness already upon me. Cold and shivering, yet covered in pungent sweat, I finished off the methadone then shakily made my way downstairs to the bathroom to take a piss. At first I thought I'd walked in on the big black guy taking a bath, and I stepped backwards quickly, my hasty apologies hanging in the silent air like a swarm of hovering flies. But then the split-second glimpse I had caught of him registered itself in my brain: something wasn't quite right — the bathwater was a murky brown colour, while the man was motionless, apparently floating, just beneath the surface of the water.

I opened the door again and peeked inside, and this time I was sure. If a black man can be blue, then he was blue, almost dead in the water, with only a faint bubbling around the nose and lips where they broke the surface to indicate that he was still alive. He'd shit himself while he was unconscious, and the yellow-brown water had left a tide mark of scum around the sides of the tub as the level rose and fell slightly with the OD victim's unanchored body. I stood there in shock looking down at him, unable to move or act, a prisoner in a frozen, but fleeting, moment of time. The house was silent — no-one was awake yet — and as I stared, I found myself focusing on the froth around his nose and mouth, the sunlight shining on the bubbles that occasionally burst there. Despite his build, and the massive bone plates of his shaven skull, he reminded me of a runny-nosed child who has been crying, blubbering through the snot and tears, waiting to be coddled and comforted for some unjustified wrong that he feels has been inflicted upon him. Big as he was, he looked oddly vulnerable, naked and afloat in his own diluted shit; also younger now that the hard facial lines had relaxed and softened with his unconscious state — almost as if he were the innocent kid brother of his own streetwise and brutal self. And I experienced some kind of vision, a synaptic flash that exploded in a rapid succession of images, revealing to me, in tortuous and precise detail, all the stages of his life so far: the pain and everyday humiliations of childhood; his first sexual encounters; the confusion and anxiety of teenage love; later, the women he had fucked, beaten and exploited; his time in prison; the thefts, robberies and murders he had committed. It was as though our wires had somehow become crossed and, as his physical life trickled slowly away, that one part of his soul, or spirit, had jumped across the intervening space and invaded me, like a parasite or virus abandoning the host body it has cor-rupted and consumed, homing in unswervingly on some new, relatively untapped source of nourishment. Suddenly, I seemed to possess, or was possessed by, an entire catalogue of images that were not mine: a host of memories and sensations that came from the inside of someone else's skull, that raged within me like a swarm of angry wasps or some random electrical charge that I had unconsciously attracted. Just for one moment, I understood everything perfectly, and as I turned to go I looked down for one last time on this poor, abandoned carcass, floating in its sea of execration. And I realised, with a sudden, total and illuminative clarity, that this other was also me, that just as surely as I was playing host to his past lives, he too had welcomed me into the flickering and dying light of his own unconscious brain. And in that same instant, I forgave myself for all my sins and transgressions, as I forgave those who had sinned and transgressed against me, and for one fractured, blinding moment I knew what love was, both for myself and for the other. Reaching down into the stinking brown mess, in which traces of shit and vomit now floated to the surface, I pulled the plug from its hole and allowed the foul water to drain away with a horribly evocative gurgling sound.

I lifted the man up as best I could, sliding his body along the residue of slime that coated the bottom of the porcelain tub. At least now he was in a sitting position, with his arms draped over each side of the bath to prevent him from sliding back down again. I tried to bring him round by slapping his face, but he was too far gone for this to work. As it was impossible for me to lift him alone, I decided to go for help, and crossing the first floor landing I banged loudly on Cissy's door. This was her work, after all, and the least she could do was to clean up her own mess.

After several loud knocks, I heard signs of life coming from within the room and eventually the door was opened — just enough to reveal Cissy's fogged and befuddled eyes, her crazy fright-wig of hair and the shoulders of the long, white night-dress she seemed always to be wearing these days.

"What the fuck do you want? It's not even ten thirty yet . . . an' anyway, I haven't got any gear to sell, we did it all last night. So just piss off, can't you, an' let me get some kip."

Her cold and fucked-up manner sucked the light right out of me, and all the old hatred and poisons came flooding right back in. I struggled to control the rising tide of rage and violence that threatened to overwhelm me at any moment.

"There's a friend of yours has been blowin' bubbles in the bathtub all night. He's just about snuffed it, but if you call an ambulance quick you might still save him. That's if you're in the least bit interested . . ."

Cissy looked totally confused for a moment, then she opened the door wider, stepped across the landing and went into the bathroom. Behind her, in the room, I could see four or five tangled bodies, laid out at various angles across the floor and bed, with an assortment of spoons, syringes, soot-blackened silver foil and overflowing ashtrays lying on every available surface. I heard Cissy's sharp intake of breath from the bathroom, and a whispered, "Oh Jesus, Brian . . . ;" then she was running back across the landing, screaming at the top of her voice, "Carol, Carol, wake up for fuck's sake, it's Brian, he's OD'd, we've got to get help, quick!" She pushed past me into the room and shook Carol roughly to wake her.

"Come on, come on, wake up you dozy cow — Brian's OD'd, we've got to call an ambulance!"

Carol groggily raised her head. She didn't seem to know where she was or what was happening at all; but Cissy slapped her around the face a few times, then pulled her protesting and uncomprehending out of the door and into the bathroom, where the sight of her half-dead boyfriend had the desired effect of bringing her to her senses.

"Oh my Gawd, Brian, Brian," she wailed in a piercing cockney lament, her voice cracked and shrill, her hands clutching at the air as if there were some invisible enemy, or demon, she was battling with.

"Brian, Brian, oh Brian, wake up please . . . oh fuck, what am I gonna do, oh Jesus, Jesus, Jesus . . ."

"Shut up, you stupid bitch, you'll wake the whole bloody street! Listen, we've got to call an ambulance, but I've got to ditch my things first, otherwise we'll all get busted. No, you go and call the ambulance, I'll tidy up an' try to keep Brian alive — no, I'll go, fuck all the stuff, he's gonna die if we're not quick . . ." And with that, Cissy dashed back into her room, pulled on a coat and was out of the door in seconds. Carol was holding onto Brian's wrist, still keening and wailing hopelessly, while gradually the other people in Cissy's room were beginning to come around, and were starting to realise that something was seriously amiss. Quickly, two of them were down the stairs and out of the front door; but a third did stay with Carol and began to massage Brian's heart, while all the time she continued to moan and cry. Obviously, after he'd OD'd, someone had put Brian into a bath full of cold water to try and revive him, before either leaving the premises or going back into Cissy's room and passing out. They must all have been so loaded when it happened that things had got confused — possibly Cissy and Carol were already unconscious, and if they had woken at any point they probably thought that Brian had just gone to the toilet, or maybe to the all-night garage for cigarettes, and had simply forgotten about him. Now Carol was wailing and weeping for her lost love, a blood-chilling, desolate sound, and as I made my way slowly back up the stairs, I wasn't sure if what I'd just witnessed was low tragedy or high farce.

· · ·

The ambulance came about twenty minutes later and they carried Brian out of the door on a stretcher, his massive body covered with a blanket and an oxygen mask on his face. The fucker must be as strong as an ox to still be alive after overdosing then spending five or six hours in a bath full of icy water. Whether he'll pull through and, if he does, whether he'll have permanent brain damage or not is anyone's guess. Carol was still crying and moaning, her hair tangled and her make-up all smudged, as she got into the ambulance with Brian. She continued holding onto his hand the whole time, as if he were some kind of anchor, the only thing in her life that could save her from floating off into the storm-ridden waves of chaos and mayhem that would otherwise overwhelm her completely.

A couple of cops also showed up to interview people and take notes, in case Brian died, I suppose. Of course, by the time they arrived everything had been stashed, and as far as we all knew he had brought his own drugs with him (which was true, as a matter of fact). There had been a party, he had locked himself in the bathroom to shoot up, and was later found slumped on the toilet seat with the needle still in his arm. He'd been put into a bath of cold water to try and revive him. That was all any of us knew, end of story.

They weren't really interested. As far as they were concerned, we were just another report to be filed: whacked-out, junkie, low-life scum. If we wanted to kill ourselves with smack, then it was nothing to them, one way or the other. Of course, it meant more paperwork and having to verbally communicate with species of human life they probably found depressing and disgusting — but this, after all, was what they were paid to do. They were the clerks, snoops and garbage disposal men of the huge, relentless machine that has us all by the balls, paid to go around and sweep up the wreckage: all the weak, damaged pieces of human debris that the machine shits out of its vast and pullulating arsehole; all of those who can't, or won't, comply; all those who refuse to, or can't, find an acceptable way of accommodating themselves to its needs and requirements. One of the cops did become interested in the novel and original way in which our electricity supply was connected, and began to ask some awkward questions. But then their radios crackled into life and they were called off to some other emergency, blue lights flashing and sirens wailing, leaving a gaggle of neighbours outside on the pavement, talking amongst themselves and looking up at the house with mingled expressions of curiosity and disapproval.

Now it's late evening, and I'm sitting here alone in my room, wondering what the fuck to do and where it all goes from here. Cissy locked herself away right after the cops left and hasn't been seen since, and to be honest I don't care what she does from now on. Me, I'm through with this junkie life. I can't afford and can't be bothered to wait around any longer, hoping that she will change, or that I will change, and that somehow we'll get back together again. I'm bailing out of this stinking ship, and she'll just have to take her chances, the same as me.

Just how I'm going to do this is a moot point, though — after all, I've tried before and nothing has kept me clean so far. I've gone cold turkey, I've reduced gradually, I've been on maintenance, I've been in a rehabilitation clinic. None of it has worked up to now. The problem is memory: as soon as the immediate pain of withdrawal has passed, you tend to forget about it and start hungering for the high again — you have the illusion that, somehow, you can experience the pleasure without the pain, if only you handle things correctly this time around. But in my experience you always end up back at the same point, whichever way you choose, and however long it takes: sick, miserable and alone, without money and with no drugs. I think that maybe, finally, my body has begun to realise this. I mean, every junkie in the world knows that shooting heroin is stupid and self-destructive; but smack is such a powerful and physically addictive drug that the rational part of your brain has no chance at all against the lure that it holds over your body — the situation is similar to that of a teacher endlessly lecturing a rebellious child, and quite simply it just doesn't work. But I think that if there is such a thing as cellular memory, within the bones, skin and tissue of the body itself, then finally the message might have started to get through. I just feel so heartily sick, tired and bored of the whole fucking deal that I might even succeed, this time, in staying off smack for good.

I've decided to pull one last stunt on poor, old, long-suffering Doc. Mitchell. I'm going to tell him that I have to go away for six weeks to America, for family reasons, then persuade him to write me a script for the entire amount I'll need over that period, which should be well over two thousand mls. I'll even ask him for a covering note to give to the U.S. immigration people in case I get searched. This will make it sound doubly convincing, and I'm sure he'll give me the stuff because he believes me and sees me as his star pupil — I can read what's in his mind, and I tell him exactly the type of psycho-confessional crap he wants to hear. After pulling this little scam, I'll sell off most of the methadone because I'm flat broke right now and I need to buy myself a bit of time in which to get clean. I can't afford a private clinic, so I'll just have to hope that someone gives me a break and a place to stay while I sweat it out over the next month or two. I'm going to reduce quickly — five mls. every three days — so from my present level of fifty a day down to zero should take about a month. Then, after I've stopped, I'll just sweat it out for however long it takes — fuck it, it can't be any worse than what I've been through before, and this time I'm doing it for myself, because I want to quit, not because someone else is telling me to, or because I want something in return.

As for how I'll cope with my re-entry into "normal" society — well, who can tell? Sometimes, I look at all these maniacs going to work each day, with their closed, miserable faces, and I really wonder if it's me who is crazy, or them. I mean, do they just appear to be sleepwalking along a treadmill to their deaths, or do they actually know something that I don't? Of course, if they do then the joke is on me — but I really don't think they do. I think it's just a case of everyone getting sucked into the machine, one way or another, and before they realise it, becoming trapped and locked into a regime that everyone claims to hate, but which they are actually addicted to: you want nice, fashionable clothes, so you can look good and be attractive to other people; you want access to news and information, because knowledge is power and you need it to succeed; you want to buy a house in a good neighbourhood, where you can feel secure and at ease with the world; you want a fast modern car with all the latest gadgets, so you can travel from A to B in comfort, in the shortest possible time; you want fax machines, answer machines, mobile phones, computers — things which are supposed to make life easier and less complicated, but which, of course, have exactly the opposite effect. And if you don't want these things, then certainly you'll be regarded by the majority of people as some kind of cretin or social misfit. And if life as a latter-day tribal outcast doesn't appeal, then you'll have to find a job that will earn you enough money to buy these things, and this job will be more, or less, demeaning depending on your level of education and/or family connections. Alternatively, you can start your own small business and put yourself in hock to the banks, become one more cog in the bigger machine and be, in turn, either a provider of jobs or an exploiter of labour, depending on which way you choose to look at things. But whatever the case, you will be some kind of functionary, fulfilling a role in a society that you neither understand, nor particularly feel a part of. And then the kids come along, and of course they want things too: they also have their own system of status symbols programmed into them at an ever earlier age — expensive trainers, computer games, CD players, etc. etc. — and the image-makers and ad-men have been so successful here, that if you don't buy your child all the things that the kid down the street has, then you stand a good chance of giving him or her irreparable psychological damage, an inferiority complex for life. And so the machine tightens its grip, you get sucked in deeper and deeper, and the only way you can stand it is to laugh it all off and pretend that you have "grown up" and accepted "the facts of life." It's not simply stupidity — it's just that everybody is in the same boat, and therefore some kind of silent compact has been made so that people don't feel so bad about themselves and about the way things in general are going.

I hate the fuckers who supposedly control this machine, who reap the benefits and look down from the heights with deep satisfaction, and it gives me great pleasure each time they fuck up and increasingly expose themselves to scrutiny. But in seeking to be neither sheep nor wolf I've actually ended up by becoming a cockroach — so where do I go from here? There has to be some other way besides compliance or callous exploitation — (out-and-out rejection and rebellion having led me to where I am now) — some kind of working around and between things, of finding and making contact with people who have similar ideas, but have found some way to exist creatively at the margins without succumbing to negativity and despair. I guess it's a hard, lonely road to travel, and you will have to live by your wits and instincts if you choose to take it — no company pension or health schemes; no pay-scales or annual increments — but I suppose being a junkie for ten years is good training for this.

I'll second-guess the power-addicts and control-freaks, the greed-heads and anal-retentive manager types all the way down the fucking line; and even if it means I end up shadow-boxing my own reflection in an infinitely receding hall of mirrors, it's got to be more interesting and rewarding than what I'm doing right now. But for the moment, I'm just going to concentrate on getting well. Once the drugs are out of my system, I'll teach myself how to think and feel again; and then I'll take a long, hard look, and see how the world appears from the other side of the street.

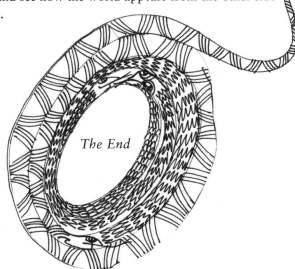

The End

PHIL SHOENFELT was born in Bradford, England, in 1952. After colliding with the London punk scene in the mid-1970s, he moved to New York where he lived and played in several bands, such as Khmer Rouge, and was active on the downtown Manhattan arts scene. Returning to London in 1984, he continued making music until encroaching heroin addiction brought a temporary halt to all such activity. Finally kicking the habit after eleven years, he embarked upon a solo career and in 1995 moved to Prague, where he currently lives. In recent years he has produced several CDs of his music on various independent labels: solo; with his band Southern Cross; and with the Berlin-based The Fatal Shore. *Junkie Love* is Shoenfelt's second book. His first, a collection of poetry and song lyrics titled *The Green Hotel*, was published in 1998.

JUNKIE LOVE by phil shoenfelt is published by twisted spoon press: p.o. box 21 – preslova 12, 150 21 prague 5, czech republic, www.twisted-spoon.com • illustrated by jolana izbická • set in sabon • design by chaim • printed & bound in the czech republic by pb tisk • distributed to the trade in north america by scb distributors: 15608 south new century drive, gardena, ca, 90248, info@scbdistributors.com / www.scbdistributors.com / toll free: 1-800-729-6423

SECOND PRINTING